MW01124724

THE RISE OF THE DEMON PRINCE

BOOK TWO OF THE COUNTERFEIT SORCERER

A NOVEL BY ROBERT KROESE

PROLOGUE

I stood watch the night the city burned.

From my vantage point at the highest platform affixed to Apa Tornya, the tallest tower in Nagyvaros, I could see every corner of that vast and teeming city. I would like to report that I was distracted when the fire began—that I dozed for a moment, or that I was looking the wrong way—and that by the time I saw it, it was too late, but that would be a lie. Except for the pale glow of the full moon and a few candles that still burned at that late hour, the city was in darkness. I saw the fire begin, and I smiled when the eastern wind picked up. It was not a joyous smile, but rather the smile of a man who, having suffered a long time with an incurable illness, finally sees the end drawing near. When the conflagration could no longer be contained, I raised the alarm, but by that time the first cries of terror had already reached my ears. There would be no question about what I had done, and there would be no doubt as to my fate—if anyone were left alive to have me condemned.

I watched, mesmerized, as the blaze moved westward. By this time, a dozen houses had already been consumed, and people awakened by screams or smoke had begun to pour into the streets. Some had begun organizing a brigade to carry water in buckets from the well by the eastern gate, but it was a pitiful effort undertaken out of desperation. Before the first bucket of water was delivered, those on the front lines had been forced by the heat and smoke to flee. A score of homes was now ablaze, and the fire had reached the commercial district. Many of the buildings here were constructed of brick or the mysterious aggregate favored by the builders of the ancient city that predated Nagyvaros. These materials would not burn, but wooden doors, window frames, partition walls, and support beams, as well as tapestries and furnishings, provided plenty of fodder for the fire. Still, the fire's progress slowed a bit; perhaps if they'd gotten more warning the people of the city might have arrested the blaze there, but they were too slow and too disorganized. The fire reached the dense foliage of the Municipal Gardens and quickly tripled in size. Nothing could stop it now.

As waves of heat washed over me, I wondered if I was safe at the top of Apa Tornya—not that there was anything I could do about it in any case. By the time I climbed down to the ground, the flames would have reached the base of the tower. The tower itself was an artifact of the ancient city and thus constructed from the impervious aggregate, but a large timber palisade had been constructed around its base. It would be fitting if I were overcome by heat or smoke, but I suspected I would not be so lucky. No, I would live to see that mighty city razed to the ground, and I would live to see the horrors that came after. I would walk the ash-covered streets, the smoke from the smoldering ruins burning my lungs, and the other unlucky survivors would point at me as I passed and curse my name, but they would not lay a hand on me—because they would see the brand on my face, and they would know I was the only one who could save them from what came next.

The fire had now reached the buildings closest to the palisade. A wide avenue had been constructed on the eastern side of the structure partly to act as a firebreak, but it did little good. The wind carried embers to the roof of the palisade, and soon a dozen little fires were burning. Men scurried about the roof, stomping out the fires as best they could, but they couldn't keep up. The men jumped from the roof and then did their best to flee. Some had broken bones in the fall and were unable to get away in time. They lay on the ground or tried to crawl away but were quickly overcome by the heat or the smoke. Embers landed on some of them, setting their clothes ablaze, but the men didn't move.

As the palisade erupted in flame, the heat came at me in waves, almost unbearable in their intensity. I cried out, and I imagined throwing myself from the tower into the cold water of the Zold. But this was a fantasy: the river was nearly a mile away, on the far western side of the city. The fire would not stop until it reached it. There were no bridges on this part of the Zold; only those lucky enough to get aboard one of the barges would escape the flames. As the heat grew even more intense, I considered throwing myself from the tower anyway. Apa Tornya was nearly three hundred feet tall; I would die instantly on impact.

But this, I knew, was not my fate either. I would not be spared the sight of the destruction of Nagyvaros nor of the hellish heat that accompanied it. My eyes burned from the smoke, but I forced myself to keep them open, to take it all in. Nearly a third of the city was now ablaze, and the spires cast long, harsh shadows across the Zold and the plains beyond. The spectacle was eerily beautiful; from this height I could almost imagine the people scurrying frantically to escape the flames were only mice or insects. But the wind, carrying their screams, spoiled the illusion. *You did this*, the wind howled at me. *You destroyed Nagyvaros.*

I wanted to protest, to say it wasn't true, but the words caught in my parched throat. Tears poured down my cheeks and the heat seared my skin. I backed away from the railing, putting my back against the stone wall, but there was no relief: the unbearable heat was everywhere. It was as if the fire were inside me, consuming me from the inside out. I tore off my clothing, but nothing helped. I wanted to die but could not. The only hope I had was that the fire would eventually have to pass. But I was in such agony that time seemed to have lost all meaning. Seconds seemed like hours. I opened my mouth to scream but could not make a sound.

Then a shadow passed over me, and there was some relief. Someone had moved between me and the flames. A familiar voice spoke: "It's all right, old friend. The worst is over. Drink a little of this."

I felt the mouth of a bottle at my lips. Cold water poured into my mouth and down my chin. I wanted to weep for joy, but my tears had all been spent.

"Easy, that's enough for now." I knew the voice but could not place it. It was someone I knew, someone I trusted. The bottle, I thought. Something about the bottle jogged my memory.

"Rodric?" I croaked.

"Ah, you recognize my voice. Then I suppose you haven't lost your wits entirely."

"The flames," I gasped. "You'll burn!"

Rodric chuckled. "I wish. It's as cold as a troll's tits tonight."

I opened my eyes and realized I was lying in bed, with my head and shoulders propped up on pillows. Rodric sat on the bed next to me; behind him a fire roared in the fireplace.

I sat up. "The fire…?" I asked uncertainly.

"I paid a few more ermes for extra wood tonight," Rodric said. "The healer said not to let the room get too cold, even though you've been burning up for three days. Anyway, it seems the fever has broken at last."

"Fever," I repeated dumbly. "Then the city… Nagyvaros is safe?"

Rodric gave me a pained look. "Oh, not by a long shot," he said.

CHAPTER ONE

Having not had a bite to eat in three days, I was famished. Rodric managed to fetch me some bread and sausages, as well as some weak wine. While I waited, I gulped down the rest of the water. Outside the window, it was dark. There were two other small beds in the room; on the farthest one slept a curled-up figure whom I recognized as my other traveling companion, the orphaned boy, Vili.

I couldn't eat much, but I was able to sate the worst of my hunger. Rodric fetched a washbasin while I ate, and I stripped off my sweat-stained clothes and gave myself a perfunctory bath. By the time I'd finished, I was exhausted. Rodric had meanwhile changed my filthy bed sheets, and I lay down again and slept for some time. When I woke again, it was light outside, and Vili and Rodric were gone. I dressed myself and then went down the to the common room and got some breakfast. The owner of the Lazy Crow, a haggard old woman named Dimka, seemed surprised to see me up and about.

"Thought you was a goner," she said, without much indication of either interest or sympathy.

"I was," I replied. "But then I came back."

She shrugged and went back to washing dishes. My mind was filled with questions, but I doubted Dimka would be much help, so I ate and drank and waited for Rodric to return.

Rodric returned a little before noon and we ensconced ourselves in a booth in the corner of the inn. I saw now that Rodric had shaved and cleaned himself up since we met at the road; except for the bags under his eyes, he looked almost his old self.

"How do you feel?" Rodric asked.

"Like I'm on the wrong side of a tombstone," I said. "How long has it been since…?" I vaguely remembered arriving at the inn with Rodric and Vili, but I couldn't be sure how much time had passed before the fever hit.

"It will be a week tomorrow," Rodric said. "You slept for most of the first three days, and then spent the next three days feverish and delirious. Vili was afraid you weren't going to make it."

"And you?"

"I know you're too damned stubborn to die. Besides, we have a demon to stop."

"Voros Korom," I said, the memory coming unbidden to my mind.

"And his following of fractious phantoms."

"I take it there has been no sign of them since they headed east?"

"None. I suppose it's too much to hope for that the demon has changed his mind?"

"I'm afraid so. Voros Korom will not rest until he has destroyed Nagyvaros."

"Then why did he turn away from the city a week ago?"

"I have a guess," I said, "but I will need to consult with an expert to be certain."

Rodric frowned. "You speak of Eben the warlock."

"How do you know of Eben?"

"You've been ranting about him—and Beata, and Radovan, and someplace called Veszedelem—for three days. Vili helped me fill in the gaps. Eben is the one who gave you that brand?"

I touched my face. I'd nearly forgotten about my disfigurement. "That's right."

"He is dead?"

"That's a bit of a gray area. The body he occupied when I first encountered him was dying, so he took Beata's. When Beata died, he fled to the shadow world— Veszedelem. His spirit remains there, suspended between life and death."

"Sorcerers are not to be trusted."

"That is, in general, a good rule."

"But you're going to consult with him anyway?"

"I must. I hate him, but he is the only one who knows how to stop Voros Korom."

"Or so he wants you to believe."

I sighed. "I can see that you are not going to be satisfied with simple answers. Would it help if I told you the whole story from the beginning?"

"It would be a start," Rodric said. "But hold off until Vili returns. Then you can tell us both at once."

We sat and talked about our time in the Scouting Corps for a while, and then Rodric filled me in on what he'd been doing since he deserted. Vili walked into the inn about an hour later. He expressed how happy he was to see me ambulatory and lucid, and I thanked him and Rodric for making that possible. Then I told my two companions everything that had happened since I'd gone to meet Beata at the Lazy Crow over six years earlier.

I told them about the cloaked man who was being pursued by the acolytes of Turelem, and how he had taken Beata hostage. I told them how I'd intervened to save Beata, and how the cloaked man had seized me and I'd been transported to the shadow world. I told them about losing consciousness and waking up in a cart bound for Nincs Varazslat, the prison for sorcerers. I told them about learning of the brand on my face, my trial and conviction, the six long years I spent in that prison, and my release at the hands of a mysterious benefactor. I told them about finding Beata only to learn that it was really Eben the warlock. I told them about finding Beata in the shadow world and pleading with the demon Szarvas Gyerek to let her die. I told them about Radovan summoning Voros Korom in order to destroy Nagyvaros. And I told them about how I'd trapped Eben in the shadow world, and how he'd forced me to take on the task of defeating Voros Korom.

"Then you believe Eben really does want to save Nagyvaros?" Rodric asked.

"I do."

"For what purpose?"

"That is a very good question," I said, "and I'm afraid I do not know the answer yet. Given what I know of Eben, I can say with some certainty that he is not motivated by altruism."

"Then is it not dangerous to ally ourselves with him? Even if you are correct in your assessment, and if we somehow succeed in stopping Voros Korom, how do we know we are not saving Nagyvaros only to deliver it over to some greater evil?"

"We don't," I replied. "But the city will be destroyed for certain if we do not stop Voros Korom."

"And what about the sorcerer who tried to kill you?" Vili asked. "Is he truly dead, or is he also trapped in the shadow world?"

"I am far from an expert on such things, but I believe Radovan to be dead. That is one matter on which I hope to get clarification from Eben."

"Do you know why Radovan wished to destroy Nagyvaros?" Rodric asked.

I shook my head.

"It seems there is a great deal we do not know," Rodric said.

"All the more reason to consult with Eben."

"Perhaps Eben can tell you what happened to my parents," Vili said.

Rodric raised an eyebrow at me.

"Vili's parents disappeared in the Maganyos Valley," I explained. Vili bit his lip and looked away. I saw from the look in Rodric's eyes that he understood what this meant: before Voros Korom led them away to the east, the wraiths haunted Maganyos Valley.

"The more I learn of this whole business," Rodric said, "the less I like it. Vili, it brings me no joy to say this, but your parents are gone. I know little of such things, but I saw that procession of wraiths across the plain. No man or woman could stand against such monsters."

Vili shook his head and opened his mouth to speak, but the words wouldn't come out. His eyes glistened with tears. I put my hand on his shoulder. "You misunderstand, Rodric," I said. "Vili knows his parents are gone. He only wishes to make sure that they are at peace, and not...." I trailed off, not wishing to speak the idea aloud. Each of the scores of wraiths that followed Voros Korom was composed of the tormented souls of hundreds of people. I had promised Vili we would make sure his parents were not among them.

Rodric flushed. "I am a fool," he said. "Vili, I beg your forgiveness. I had assumed you were acting out of childish naivete, but I see now that you are only doing what you must. I can only hope that if, Turelem forbid, I am ever faced with such a challenge, I shall be so bold."

Vili nodded, smiling grimly.

"You are far too hard on yourself, old friend," I said. "The truth is, you are the only one of us who has taken on this quest willingly. Vili and I have little choice, but you have volunteered for this burden. And I will remind you that it is not too late for you to back out."

"And spend the rest of my days trying to kill the memories of my cowardice with wine?" Rodric asked. "No, my path is here with you. But how is it that you do not have a choice, Konrad? I understand that you would save Nagyvaros if you could, but this is not your city. No one would blame you if you fled as far and as quickly from Voros Korom as you could."

I managed a smile. "It seems that I glossed over my agreement with Eben, and in doing so inadvertently painted myself as more heroic than I am. Although I would like to believe I would do what I could to save Nagyvaros in any case, the fact is that my soul is beholden to a demon named Szarvas Gyerek. Were it not for Eben's intervention, I too would be lost in the shadow world. But my salvation came at a cost: I am committed to keep Voros Korom from destroying Nagyvaros."

"And if you fail?"

"I will spend the next thousand years in Veszedelem, doing the bidding of Szarvas Gyerek."

"Why would you enter into such a bargain?"

"I did not do so willingly. In order to free Beata from her torment, I pledged my blood to Szarvas Gyerek. I was near death, and Szarvas Gyerek would have taken my soul. Eben volunteered to take my place, on the condition that I stop Voros Korom."

Rodric sighed in exasperation. "I see that I never should have let you go off on your own. I thought I'd had a rough time of it, but I see now that you've gotten yourself into more trouble than I'd imagined possible. Rest assured, though, that my bow is at your service, for whatever that's worth."

"It's worth quite a bit," Vili ventured, "judging from your treatment of those bandits on the road."

Rodric waved his hand in embarrassment. "Luck was with me that day. It was only the hand of Turelem that kept me from skewering one of you by accident."

I smiled but didn't argue. Rodric was the greatest archer I'd ever known or heard about, but he lived in constant fear that his gift would leave him. When the fear became too much, he drowned it in wine, but when we were together he abstained out of a desire not to disappoint me. So while he maintained that he'd pledge himself to our cause of his own volition, in a sense he was just as bound to it by fate as Vili and I.

"You say you released Beata from her torment," Rodric said, desperate to change the subject. "Do you mean she is at peace?"

"Beata is dead," I said, surprising myself with the lack of emotion in my voice. "By the time I found her, the bond between her soul and her body was too weak for her to return. There was nothing left to do but release her from the shadow world."

"You mustn't blame yourself, Konrad," Rodric said. "It was Eben who put her there."

"I know. I swore to kill him for it."

"And yet he still lives."

"In a manner of speaking. Without a vessel to occupy, he is trapped in the shadow world. It is a fitting punishment for what he did to Beata."

"You speak the words without conviction."

I shook my head tiredly. "It is a strange business, dealing with sorcerers. As soldiers, we became accustomed to death, and perhaps we deluded ourselves into thinking that we understood it. We condemn a man to death and think that the matter is settled, content with the assurance that if there is anything beyond death, the gods will deal with the souls of the deceased as they see fit. But now the veil has been drawn back, and I see the face of Eben laughing at me."

"But you wish to take his counsel."

"I will speak with him, in order to learn what I must to defeat Voros Korom."

"And when that is done?"

"Mere death is too good for Eben the Warlock. I swear to you, I will see his soul obliterated."

CHAPTER TWO

I spent most of the remainder of the day resting. Although it was only my mind that would travel to the shadow world, physical weakness would manifest as mental weakness, and it would not do to let Eben see me in a compromised condition. Eben and I shared a desire to save Nagyvaros, but I suspected our plans would diverge sharply once that had been accomplished—and it would be foolish to think Eben was not plotting for advantage even now.

After breakfast the next morning, I closed myself in the room in the inn, forbidding Rodric and Vili to enter for the next hour. The meeting was unlikely to take that long, as time passed much more slowly in the shadow world than it did in ours, but I thought I might need the time to recover.

I sat on my bed and removed the bandage from my hand. The wound had sealed, but it took only a slight pull on the skin to cause a small pool of blood to well up in my palm. I closed my eyes and allowed my mind to drift to the shadow world. Finding myself once again on the vast gray plain, facing the ominous black keep called Sotetseg, I held my hand out and allowed the blood to drip to the ground. As it struck the soil, waves of energy swept outward like ripples on a pond. In the distance, I heard the howls of the ravenous beasts in the mountains. They sensed the power of a sorcerer's blood and would soon begin to pour onto the plain after me. I moved quickly toward the keep, occasionally allowing a drop of blood to fall to the ground in front of me. I did not know why I always appeared at that particular place on the plain, but I had learned that my blood would create a path that I could traverse to the keep. Unfortunately, it also attracted monsters.

I knew from experience, though, that the monsters stayed in the mountains unless lured onto the plain, and that I could reach the guard tower in front of the keep before they could cross the plain toward me. Whether I could get inside the guard tower was another matter. If the mysterious "Masters" who ruled the keep had made alterations to their defenses since the last time I'd visited, I might find myself trapped outside to face the ravenous hordes.

But I was relieved to find, when I reached the guard tower, that the impression of a man's hand appeared as before, just to the right of the door. I could now hear the snarls and growls of the creatures rumbling across the plain behind me. I pressed my palm against the impression, and the door swung open. I slipped inside, placed my other hand on the impression on the inside wall, and breathed a sigh of relief as the door began to swing closed. None too soon, either: a second after I heard the bolt slide into place, a half-dozen creatures slammed into the door.

The first floor of the tower was empty, as far as I could tell in the dim light. Several large stone pillars supported the upper levels; around the periphery wound a stone staircase. I climbed to the third level, where dim light from the angled slits in the walls illuminated the figure of a man standing in the center of the room. He faced outward from the castle; from his vantage point, he could observe the entire plain outside the moat. Behind him, in the direction of the castle, was a wooden door. A key protruded from its keyhole.

I did not know the watchman's name, nor why he had been sentenced to this fate, forced by some enchantment to stand, unmoving, eternally surveying the dismal plain. All I knew of him came from a song once sung to me by the mysterious man called Bolond while I was in the dungeon of Nincs Varazslat:

Blind and deaf the watchman waits
never opening the gates
but to the one he once betrayed

until the debt at last is paid

"Bolond commands you to open the door," I said.

The man turned toward me and nodded. He turned away and walked the short distance to the door. He put his fingers on the key and turned it until the lock clicked, then put his hand on the knob, turned it, and pulled the door open. He stepped aside, his hand still on the knob.

On the other side of the door was a chasm, perhaps a hundred feet across, whose bottom was lost in fog and shadow. The chasm acted as a moat around the foreboding keep. As I watched, fog roiled out of the chasm and gradually solidified into the form of a bridge.

I stepped onto the bridge, and the silent watchman closed the door behind me. I strode across. The portcullis on the other side raised as I approached, and I went into the castle.

I found myself in a large vaulted hall into which little light penetrated. It seemed to be deserted. I proceeded to a door at the far end and threw it open to reveal a rectangular courtyard open to the dismal gray sky above. Several doors and open passageways led from it. I headed down the one that led to the area below the keep where the demon Szarvas Gyerek resided, but I was soon lost in a labyrinth of tunnels and passageways. Knowing that I could with minimal effort return to my physical body, I did not fear the possibility of being unable to find my way out, but wandering these passageways at random would do me no good. Further, I did not know what other creatures lurked below the keep, and I did not know if my pact with Szarvas Gyerek would keep me safe from them. Could the creatures here harm me even though my body was safe back at the Lazy Crow? I did not know. I had no weapons; I had learned that metal objects could not be transported to the shadow world. Perhaps I could have taken a wooden club or cudgel, but it was too late for that now, and in any case I didn't like my chances facing a demon with a cudgel. If I saw the creature coming, I could flee the shadow world, but if I were surprised, I might not have a chance.

I came to a square chamber about twenty paces across, dimly lit by a torch burning in a sconce centered in the wall across from the doorway through which I'd entered. To my left and right were passageways that led into the darkness. I moved across the chamber and turned to put my back against the wall; the torch now burned just over my left shoulder. Satisfied that if some loathsome beast came bounding toward me out of the darkness I would have time to force my consciousness back to my physical form, I shouted, "Szarvas Gyerek! Show yourself!"

My words echoed down the corridors and died. For some time I listened but heard nothing. I opened my mouth again. "Szarvas Gyerek!" I cried. "It is I, Konrad. I have come to consult with—"

"Shhh!" hissed someone from the dark passage to my left. A few seconds later a cloaked man emerged from the darkness: Eben the warlock. Hatred surged inside of me. It was all I could do not to throw myself on him and tear him limb from limb. The only thing that restrained me was the suspicion that it would do no good. Eben no longer possessed a physical body; he lived in Veszedelem as spirit. I suspected that his projection would evaporate as soon as I lay a hand on him. No, to truly kill Eben I would need to be patient and learn everything I could about the shadow world.

"Quiet, you fool!" Eben snapped as he approached. "He'll hear you!"

"Szarvas Gyerek?" I said. "That was the idea. Are you not obliged to do the demon's bidding? I assumed that to speak with you, I would need to get permission from him."

"Technically, yes," Eben said. "But Szarvas Gyerek cannot watch me constantly, and it is better if he does not know of our meeting."

"You plot against him already?"

"Already!" Eben scoffed. "It's been two years! This way." He marched across the chamber to the passage on my right. I followed.

Two years. I hadn't had a chance to think about it, but of course he was right. A hundred times as much time had passed in the shadow world as in Orszag. It had only been a week for me—most of which I'd spent unconscious—but Eben had now been in the service of Szarvas Gyerek for two years. Two years to plan for my appearance and to plot his escape. For I had no doubt that Eben did not intend to serve his full sentence of a millennium doing the bidding of Szarvas Gyerek. I could only hope he had devoted some of his time to figuring out how to defeat Voros Korom.

We spent several minutes making our way through the maze of passageways. Our course seemed random to me—sometimes going left, sometimes right, sometimes climbing, sometimes descending, but I got the impression that we were gradually going deeper below the keep. After the seventh or eighth turn, I gave up trying to memorize the way. I wasn't even certain I could have found my way back to the chamber where we'd started. Eben held no torch, but a dim light seemed to follow us as we moved through the tunnels. Some sorcery on his part, no doubt.

At last we reached a door at the end of a narrow passage that opened into a small library. It seemed disused and ill-maintained: the odor of mildew permeated the air. Eben led me to a wooden table in the center of an array of shelves that held hundreds of dusty, decaying volumes. Somewhere in the distance I heard the slow dripping of water. He muttered an incantation, and a lantern on the table came to life, illuminating the place with a greenish-yellow glow only a little brighter than the light that had brought us there. Eben sat in a chair on one side of the table, and I sat in another across from him. I think that little library with its books silently dying in the musty air may be the saddest place I have ever been.

"He will not find us here," Eben said.

"What of the other demons?"

"They are few, and the keep is vast. This library is ostensibly under Szarvas Gyerek's control, but he has no interest in it, as you can see."

"Will he not be looking for you?"

Eben shrugged. "I have made a habit of obsequious obedience, eagerly carrying out every task he assigns me. Szarvas Gyerek is a dour, solitary type, so he quickly tires of my presence. I pretend to have no interests other than serving him, and in this way have secured several hours of freedom on most days. I know these passages better than he does, and I have several hiding places like this where I can work undisturbed. I've provided him with a bell that he can ring if he wishes to summon me, so I do not have to worry about him coming to look for me."

"What are these tasks he assigns to you?" I asked. "And what is this work you are doing on your own? Is it too much to hope that you have put some effort into finding a way to stop Voros Korom?"

Eben smiled. "I will speak neither of my work for Szarvas Gyerek nor of my own activities, except those which directly concern you. Yes, I have dedicated much of my time to seeking out Voros Korom's weaknesses, but I am afraid I have come up with very little. Voros Korom alone would be a formidable adversary, but it is his entourage of wraiths that are the true danger. With the power of the brand you might be able to destroy them, but only if you are trained in how to use it. I must say, I had hoped you would return somewhat sooner."

"This is the first I've been well enough to come to the shadow world since our last meeting. I was nearly killed by Radovan, as you may recall."

"An eventuality that could have been prevented if you had listened to me."

"If I'd have listened to you, you'd have killed me yourself."

Eben smiled. "True, but Voros Korom would remain in the shadow world."

"As would Beata, whose life you stole from her. Listen to me, warlock. I have not come here to be your enthralled pupil, nor your starry-eyed protégé. You will teach me what I need to know to defeat Voros Korom, and then we are finished."

"Ah, but it is not so simple, young Konrad. One does not try on the ways of sorcery as if they were a fancy new suit of clothes to be worn once to a ball and then discarded. If you wish to defeat Voros Korom, you must become what you have pretended to be."

"I will learn what I must to save Nagyvaros and defeat Voros Korom, just as I learned what I had to in order to free Beata and put you here. Szarvas Gyerek does not own my soul, and neither will you. Now tell me how to defeat the demon."

"As you wish," said Eben with an amused smile. "Voros Korom exists in a state between Orszag and the shadow world, which is why he is able to sustain the wraiths. But to do this, he must manifest himself physically in Orszag, and when he does, he is vulnerable to attack with ordinary weapons. Do not misunderstand; he is in constant flux between the two worlds, and his skin is tougher than steel. He has the strength of a hundred men. But he is not invulnerable.

"As I say, however, the true threat is the wraiths who follow him. The wraiths too exist between Orszag and the shadow world, but in a different way than Voros Korom. Each wraith is composed of the souls of hundreds of individuals, each of whom is trapped in a sort of vortex between the two worlds. These poor souls are doomed to fight against this vortex and each other, forever trying to escape the shadow world into Orszag. They are drawn to the substance of Orszag but too weak to survive there. The sustaining energy fades the closer one gets to the mouth of the vortex, so as soon as one of the souls is on the verge of escaping, it weakens and is dragged back into the vortex by the others."

"If they only wish to escape this vortex, why did they attack me when I ventured into the ruins?"

"They sense that living people have what they lack: the energy to survive in material form. A human being carries with him a source of sustaining energy, called an akarat. The akarat is what allows a human soul to remain attached to a material form. Without it, the two would separate. The soul would dissipate and the body would wither. The souls trapped in the vortex are drawn to the energy of the akarat like moths to a lantern, but their efforts are equally futile. The trapped souls gorge themselves on the energy of the akarat, and the victim dies and its soul joins the others in the vortex."

I wanted to press Eben on the matter, but he did not know about Vili's parents. If I let on that I had a personal interest in two individuals trapped in the vortex, he might use the knowledge against me, deliberately withholding information to manipulate me. Better to be patient and let him tell me what I wanted to know of his own accord. Reluctantly, I changed the subject.

"Why did Voros Korom turn away from Nagyvaros?"

"Have you heard of Varastis? Or Magas Komaron?"

I shrugged. "Magas Komaron is a myth. A natural rock formation that those of a whimsical persuasion have made into an inaccessible fortress."

"So most believe," Eben said. "Varastis was an archaeologist working for the office of the Arcanist in Nagyvaros. The job of the Arcanist's office, as you must know, is to curate arcane knowledge and prevent it from falling into the wrong hands—which is to say, the hands of anyone but the Governor, the Arcanist, or the acolytes of Turelem. And since the Arcanist has historically been a puppet of Delivaros, it can be supposed that the Governor is, more often than not, left out of the loop.

"In any case, Varastis abruptly retired from his post and was said to have left the city. But a few years later, rumors surfaced that he had returned and established a small school somewhere in the Hidden Quarter. Varastis's students were sworn to secrecy, but it was said that he was teaching them the secrets of sorcery. At this time, sorcery was not technically illegal, but only because the acolytes held such a monopoly on arcane knowledge that such measures were unnecessary. The acolytes were convinced that Varastis had found something under the city—something left behind by the Builders—that had revealed to him knowledge that even they did not possess, and they became desperate to stop him and learn his secret. But Varastis was an expert in the law and had many friends in the government, so efforts to entrap him using existing statutes came to naught. The acolytes were forced to use all their political leverage to pressure the Assembly into passing laws expressly banning sorcery and the dissemination of arcane knowledge. Gendarmes were dispatched to the Hidden Quarter before the law was even passed, and the moment word came down that sorcery had been made illegal, they converged on the house where Varastis's school met. The acolytes knew the location only because one of Varastis's students—an ambitious man named Radovan—betrayed him. Radovan had become convinced that Varastis was keeping the greatest secrets to himself, and he hoped by ingratiating himself to the acolytes that he might infiltrate the Arcanist's office and learn Varastis's secrets.

"Many of Varastis's students were arrested and sent to Nincs Varazslat, but Varastis and a few others escaped. They fled to the east, to found a sanctuary outside of the acolytes' control. This was Magas Komaron, an impregnable fortress in the Eastern Mountains said to be constructed by the same Builders who built the ancient city that once stood at the site of Nagyvaros."

"You are saying that Magas Komaron is a real place? Not just a granite obelisk left behind by a chance fissure of rocks, but a fortress deliberately constructed on a mountain peak?"

"Were you not a scout in the janissaries? Surely you saw the beacon that glows at the top of that fortress?"

I shrugged. "It is not impossible some hermit found his way to the top of the obelisk."

"Using a path through the mountains that still has not been discovered by the best scouts in the janissaries, to say nothing of the Barbaroki? And now manages to keep a beacon perpetually lit at the summit? For what purpose? To perpetuate the myth of an ancient fortress?"

I frowned as if perplexed by the conundrum. In truth, I had never believed the mundane explanation for the beacon atop Magas Komaron, even before I'd heard Bolond sing of it in Nincs Varazslat.

"Using his arcane knowledge, Varastis found the way to Magas Komaron," Eben went on. "There, in that abandoned fortress, he established his sanctuary for sorcerers. The very night he and his disciples arrived, he commanded that a light be placed in the highest window of the fortress, and it has burned ever since, as a warning to the acolytes and a beacon for other sorcerers. It can be seen from miles away, but for years the acolytes have tried to find a way through the mountains to the tower and have failed."

"So that is why Voros Korom turned away from Nagyvaros. You sent him to Magas Komaron."

"I convinced Voros Korom that only one man presents a threat to his dominion over Nagyvaros."

"Varastis. Is it true?"

"It may be. I have never been able to learn what Varastis found under the city, and he has had twenty years since then to develop his powers. If anyone can stop Voros Korom, it is he."

"If you believed that, we would not be having this conversation."

Eben shrugged. "With enough time to prepare an offensive, Varastis might have found a way to wrest Nagyvaros from Voros Korom. But by then it would have been too late. The city would be destroyed."

"And if Voros Korom attacks Varastis at Magas Komaron?"

"Varastis will die, along with the rest of his students. Not even Varastis has a chance in a surprise attack from those wraiths."

"You sent Voros Korom to kill the only man who has a chance to stop him?"

"I had no choice. The diversion bought us six weeks. Magas Komaron is more than a week's journey from Nagyvaros. Voros Korom will likely wait until the full moon, when the wraiths are at their strongest, to attack Magas Komaron. If a week has passed in your world, then the attack will come in twelve days. Even if Varastis puts up minimal resistance, Voros Korom will need some time to recover from the battle, so I suspect that he will again wait until the full moon to attack Nagyvaros. That's six weeks, one of which you've spent in bed."

"I suppose it's only coincidental that Varastis is a rival of yours." It was only a guess, but an educated one, given what I knew of Eben.

Eben allowed a smile to play at the corner of his lips. "It is true that I will not weep at Varastis's demise. The fact remains, however, that this diversion was our only chance to save Nagyvaros. If we do not waste any more time, I may be able to train you to use the power of the brand to defend the city before Voros Korom attacks."

"Your personal grudges aside, would it not be better to go to Magas Komaron? With a fast horse, I could get there before the full moon. If I warn Varastis, perhaps we can stand against Voros Korom together."

Eben shook his head. "There is no time. A few hours to prepare will avail Varastis nothing against Voros Korom. In any case, I do not know the way." He seemed loath to admit this.

"If you do not know the way to Magas Komaron, how did you send Voros Korom there?"

"Voros Korom's strength is such that he can scale sheer rock faces that would be impassable for any man, and the wraiths cannot be stopped by any physical barrier. Voros Korom need only head directly for the beacon."

"Why does Voros Korom wish to destroy Nagyvaros?" I asked. "If I knew—"

"Blast!" Eben snapped. "There it is."

"What?"

"Ah, you cannot hear it. The bell Szarvas Gyerek uses to summon me. I must not delay, or he will begin to suspect."

"You've taught me nothing to help me defeat Voros Korom."

"There is time. Szarvas Gyerek will tire of me quickly and I will return here. It will only be a few minutes in your world. Can you find your way to this library?"

"I doubt it."

Eben sighed. "To the chamber where I met you?"

"I think so."

"All right. I will place a small bell, like the one Szarvas Gyerek uses to summon me, in the corner of the room, to the left of the torch as you enter. Return to your world, wait a short time, and then come back to that chamber. Ring the bell and count to two hundred. You will not hear the bell, but I will. If I do not appear by the time you reach two hundred, return to your world and try again shortly."

"Must I come by way of the guard tower each time? I seem to be able to return to Orszag from anyplace in the shadow world, but whenever I—"

"I will explain later," Eben said, getting to his feet. "I must attend to Szarvas Gyerek. Return when you can." With that, he was gone.

Not wishing to tarry in that sad place, I forced my awareness back to the room at the Lazy Crow. I was tired from my trip to the shadow world and my meeting with Eben, but I knew Rodric and Vili would be anxious to hear how it had gone. Besides, I had something to discuss with them before my next meeting with Eben.

I went downstairs, where Rodric and Vili waited for me in the corner booth. Rodric had not even finished the mug of watered-down ale that he'd been drinking when I went to the room.

"Have you forgotten something?" Rodric asked, as I approached.

I shook my head. "The meeting is over."

"You went upstairs not two minutes ago!"

"Time passes differently in the shadow world," I said. "Can we be ready for a week's journey by morning?"

"I can secure provisions and make sure the horses are ready," Vili said. "But are you well enough to travel?"

"I will have to be. I trust Ember to carry me gently."

"Where are we going?" Rodric asked.

"I do not feign to make such decisions on my own," I said. "We are a party of equals."

"That may be," Rodric said, "but Vili and I must depend upon you for knowledge of Voros Korom and other arcane matters. We will yield to your judgment."

Vili nodded. "We go where you decide we must go."

"Very well, friends," I said. "Although you may well come to regret that sentiment. Tomorrow morning, we set out for a place called Magas Komaron."

CHAPTER THREE

Before I went to bed, I went again to the shadow world to meet with Eben, but he did not respond to the bell. It was just as well: as much as I wanted to stop Voros Korom, I did not want Eben to get the impression I was at his beck and call, and I could use the time to think and plan before speaking with him again.

We left the inn an hour after dawn. The air was cold, but the sun shone brightly in a clear azure sky. There was no wind and no snow on the ground. We departed none too soon: Vili reported that the gendarmes had begun sweeping the Hidden Quarter, asking about a man with strange black markings on his face. Having already served six years in Nincs Varazslat for the supposed crime of sorcery, I was not anxious to meet them. Vili had not reported seeing any acolytes, which was fortunate: agents of the Governor might be reasoned with, but the acolytes cared only about maintaining their monopoly on arcane knowledge. I had known little of the Purge before meeting Eben, but what he told me rang true. I had no doubt the acolytes would be happy to see me killed trying to escape rather than bother with another trial. My legal status remained uncertain: I'd been released by the order of the Arcanist's office, but the Arcanist himself—the sorcerer Radovan—had been killed, and I suspected it was only a matter of time before those in the government uncovered the truth about him.

Vili had acquired two horses, one for him and one for Rodric. They awaited us at a stable just inside the eastern gate. The gendarmes were watching the gates, as well, but without any great conscientiousness: I huddled under a load of wool blankets in a cart that was part of a caravan destined for the military outpost called Erod Patak. Perhaps the order to watch for a man with markings on his face leaving the city had not reached the men at the gate; in general, sentries are more interested in those coming into the city than those leaving. In any case, I was not disturbed. Rodric and Vili followed the caravan about a mile out of town, leading Ember behind their own horses. I rolled out of the cart, received with aplomb a series of deprecations from the driver of the following cart, and then rejoined my comrades.

At this point I had told Rodric and Vili little more than that we were headed for Magas Komaron. This meant nothing to Vili; Rodric had raised an eyebrow, but seeing that I needed rest, did not press the matter. It was a testament to his loyalty that he thought nothing of following me to a destination that was thought to be unreachable, if not entirely fictitious. Late in the morning we came to a place where the trail widened enough to allow two horses to pass side-by-side, and he maneuvered his mount alongside of mine. Vili lagged behind; the sound of our horse's shoes crunching on the frost-covered ground covered our voices.

"Are we truly destined for Magas Komaron?" Rodric asked.

"That is the plan," I replied.

"It is not, then, merely a rock on which perches a mischievous hermit, or some mountain-dwelling variety of will-o'-the-wisp?"

"If Eben is to be believed—and I believe he was telling the truth on this matter, at least—it is an ancient fortress constructed by the same Builders who established the city that once stood on the site of Nagyvaros. It was long abandoned and now serves as a sanctuary for a sorcerer named Varastis and his followers."

"Eben instructed you to go there?"

"No. In fact, he believes the journey to be impossible."

Rodric frowned, not knowing what to make of this. I was obliged to tell him the rest of my conversation with Eben.

"Well," said Rodric, "I certainly see the wisdom of appealing to this Varastis, particularly if he is an enemy of Eben. But how do you expect to reach Magas Komaron when even Eben does not know the way?"

"This will sound foolish to you," I began.

"No doubt," Rodric agreed.

"...but I believe the answer is in a song."

"A... song?"

"When I was in Nincs Varazslat, there was another prisoner there, a man named Bolond. I thought him mad, but he entertained me with hundreds of songs that were apparently of his own invention. They seemed mostly nonsense at the time, like the sorts of songs children sing while jumping rope. I heard many of them so many times I could even now sing them by heart. I did not think they held any deeper significance until the day I went to the shadow world to rescue Beata. Beata was being held in a dungeon below a keep, which is surrounded by a deep chasm, and the way across is guarded by a lone watchman, who has been sentenced to maintain that post, unmoving, for ten thousand years. The keep and the watchman are described quite precisely in one of Bolond's songs."

"Possibly a coincidence."

"Perhaps, except for the fact that the watchman responded to Bolond's name. It was how I got into the castle."

"Then this Bolond is some sort of master sorcerer? Where is he now?"

"I do not know. I never saw him, but only heard his voice. One day his singing stopped, and I never heard him again."

"But you believe one of his songs is the key to reaching Magas Komaron."

"Yes."

"How does it go?"

I cleared my throat. I am not much of a singer, but I did my best:

No one knows what Varastis found
buried so deep under the ground
He left that night without a sound
for Magas Komaron

Setting out early on Nyarkozep

he led his disciples 'cross the wind-blasted steppe
to the path of Polgar his company kept
toward Magas Komaron

"Is that it?" Rodric asked.

"There's a bit more, but that's the part we're concerned with right now."

"Polgar is the star at the end of Szamar's Tail," Rodric said. "It passes somewhat farther south this time of year." It was only a few weeks past midwinter; Nyarkozep was on the day of the summer solstice.

"But on Nyarkozep…"

"Polgar would be directly overhead, yes. It would appear shortly after sundown in that direction, just to the right of those poplars. If you had told me earlier, I might have consulted with an astrologer and gotten us an exact heading."

"There are only so many paths through the hills. The way I figure it, we stay on this road until we reach Tabor Nev and then turn south. Maybe someone in Csakvar or one of the other villages in the foothills can tell us where Polgar appears in the east at Nyarkozep."

"You do not intend to inquire at Tabor Nev?" Rodric asked cautiously.

"Don't worry, Rodric. I'm no more eager to meet the janissaries than you are. In any case, I doubt the janissaries know anything of Polgar or Magas Komaron."

"The people at Csakvar may be equally ignorant."

"In that case, we make our best guess and press on through the hills. We were two of the best Scouts in the Eastern Army. If we can't find the way, no one can."

"It is precisely the second possibility that worries me," Rodric replied. "Assuming we find the way, can we make it to Magas Komaron before Voros Korom?"

"Voros Korom will wait until the full moon to attack, when the wraiths are at full strength. That gives us eleven days. Unless the route is very circuitous, we should arrive a day or two before the attack."

Rodric shook his head. "You are supposed to be keeping me sober, not driving me to drink. But lead on, old friend. I will follow you to the grave if need be, and dead men are the soberest of all."

We had come to a place where the trail narrowed again, and Rodric allowed his mount to slip behind mine. I was glad of this, for the conversation had drained me, and I hadn't even gotten to the more befuddling part of the song.

We made camp just before dusk. In truth, I was too exhausted to do much more than pull out my bedroll, wash down some dry biscuits with watered-down beer, and fall asleep. Vili and Rodric must have gathered wood for a fire and tended to the horses. We did not set a watch; bandits rarely ventured this far east and we had not heard of any recent Barbarok incursions onto the plain. Our greatest enemies at present were time and fatigue.

I awoke at dawn, ravenous with hunger but otherwise feeling much stronger. We breakfasted on more biscuits, jerky, and some mushrooms Vili had gathered. An hour later, we were back on our horses, heading east. At some point I would have to try again to meet Eben, but we had no time to spare. Traveling to Veszedelem took a lot out of me, and I needed all my strength.

We made good time across the plain over the next several days, which was a relief, because despite my feigned confidence, I suspected that decoding the clues in the rest of Bolond's song was going to take some time. The skies remained clear and the air was cold but still. At night, the temperature dipped below freezing, and we kept a fire burning to ward off the cold. We spent the eighth evening of our journey at an inn at Csakvar, in the foothills of the Kerepes Mountains. Our good fortune continued: an old woman there, named Nusi, claimed to have spent her youth in a Barbarok camp, where she became acquainted with the tribe's soothsayer. Soothsayers have an uncanny understanding of the movements of the stars, and Nusi had picked up a fair amount of knowledge herself. In answer to my inquiries, she pointed to a gap between two peaks and informed me that on Nyarkozep, Polgar would arise precisely between them. I thanked her and gave her an erme, which she accepted with a toothless grin.

The afternoon of the second day after leaving Csakvar, my confidence began to wane. From many miles away, the two peaks had appeared as twins, but now I saw that the one on the right was in fact many miles more distant. As we drew closer, the peak on the left grew until it towered over us while the peak that had been on the left disappeared entirely from view. The guidance that had seemed so precise from twenty leagues away was now revealed to be hopelessly vague. There was no road to speak of; just an ancient riverbed strewn with gravel and dotted with scrubby plants. The riverbed forked at countless places, and it was impossible to know where any particular branch would take us. We kept to the path of Polgar as best we could, with Vili occasionally climbing to the summit of a rocky hill in an attempt to discern the way forward. It was a slow and frustrating way to travel, and after a few hours I was forced to admit that I couldn't begin to guess the correct direction.

Nor was this our only worry: Vili advised us after one of his reconnaissance climbs that we were being followed. He had seen a lone rider, about a half mile behind us. The traveler's presence could not be coincidence; there was no known pass through the mountains this way. Either he was following us or he was himself on his way to Magas Komaron. An ordinary man would pose no threat to us, but my experience with sorcerers like Eben and Radovan suggested an abundance of caution. We would ambush the man, bind him before he had a chance to wreak any mischief, and then interrogate him.

I reluctantly ceded the key role in the ambush to Vili. I was not yet fully recovered, and the truth was that Vili was stealthier and quicker than either Rodric or myself. He crouched behind a boulder by which the traveler would be forced to pass while Rodric perched in the rocks above and I hid behind another boulder nearby. The plan was for Rodric to fire an arrow into the rocks to the man's left. The clatter of the arrow would serve as a diversion as well as a signal to Vili, who would spring from behind the boulder and pull the man from his horse. I would then leave my hiding place to assist Vili in subduing the man or getting control of his horse, depending on the exigencies of the moment.

It was a good plan, and we waited that way for the rider for over an hour. At last, thinking the rider must have passed and Rodric had fallen asleep, I stood up and signaled him. He answered with a shrug. Vili, seeing that I had left my hiding place, stood up, and Rodric clambered down the slope toward him. The three of us met on the riverbed to consider our options.

"He must have turned back," Rodric said.

"Or perhaps he has camped for the night," Vili offered.

"Or maybe," said a voice from behind us, "she anticipated your ambush and opted not to participate."

CHAPTER FOUR

A young woman in a long gray cloak came around the rocks and stopped before us. Slender fingers threw back the hood to reveal an alabaster face framed by close-cropped red hair. Rodric, who'd trained his bow the moment we heard the voice, slowly lowered it. I left my rapier in its scabbard although I was not certain the threat had passed. The woman wore her hair in the style of the acolytes of Turelem.

She turned and gave a whistle. After a moment, a small dappled gray horse—not much more than a pony—came around the rocks toward her. The woman made her way across the dry riverbed, the horse following her. As she stopped again a few paces in front of us, I saw that she was young—perhaps nineteen or twenty. It was hard to believe the acolytes would send a pretty young woman this far out into the wilderness alone—particularly only a few weeks after one of their own was murdered on the way to Nagyvaros.

"Why are you following us?" I asked.

She smiled. "Says the man with the warlock's brand on his face."

"I am no warlock," I said. "This mark was given to me against my will."

"And yet you seek the way to Magas Komaron."

"That is our business."

"As you like. You will never find it."

"That is troubling news. I understand the acolytes are experts in the matter of not finding Magas Komaron."

The woman smiled, refusing to rise to the bait. "Be that as it may, I might be of some assistance to you."

"You were sent by Delivaros to follow us in the hopes of finding the way to Magas Komaron."

"It is true that I seek the way to Magas Komaron, but the Council does not know I am here."

"You think your disobedience will be forgiven if you are successful."

"I may hope."

"And if you fail?"

"I will not return to Delivaros."

I raised an eyebrow. An acolyte renouncing her vows was no small matter. "You are very brave or very foolish to travel alone. One of your number was murdered on the way to Nagyvaros not long ago."

"An acolyte named Klotild, yes. Killed by sorcery."

"You do not fear such a fate?"

"Klotild bore an urgent warning for the Governor. I do not think my mission faces the same sort of opposition."

"A warning about what?"

"I would not tell you even if I knew."

I sighed quietly. So much for my attempts to learn why the acolyte had been murdered.

"You offer assistance," said Rodric, "but you admit you do not know the way?"

"I know the way to the Stone Door, which is apparently more than you. As you have come this far, however, I assume you have come across some clues left by someone who has been to Magas Komaron. I can only hope you know how to open the door."

Rodric glanced at me. I gave a noncommittal shrug. "If we do reach Magas Komaron, you are unlikely to be welcomed there."

"That is my concern."

"And ours, insofar as your presence in our party biases the sorcerers against us."

"The issue is moot if you never reach the place."

Rodric put his hand on my shoulder. He whispered, "She is right. We can ill afford to waste a day traipsing about in these rocks. Do you know of this Stone Door?"

"The song mentions a door, yes."

"Then perhaps she speaks the truth. The acolytes have, after all, been searching for a way to Magas Komaron for many years."

"You would have me lead an acolyte of Turelem directly to the sorcerers' refuge?"

"I don't see that we have an alternative. Let Varastis deal with her, assuming we make it there. If we arrive in time to warn him of Voros Korom, he will likely forgive us for allying with an acolyte."

I nodded and turned back to the young woman. "What is your name, acolyte?"

"I am Ilona."

"Ilona, I am Konrad. These are my companions, Rodric and Vili. We provisionally accept your offer of assistance. Beware, though, that if you attempt any mischief, we will take your horse and leave you here to find your way back to Delivaros on foot."

"I intend no mischief. You will have to extend me some trust if you expect to reach the Stone Door before sundown. We will need to leave the horses."

"Leave them here?" Rodric asked.

"We have gone some miles in the wrong direction. I did not reveal myself until I was certain you did not know the way."

"Reveal yourself!" Vili cried. "I spotted you a half-mile off!"

"As I intended."

Vili snorted, but the woman continued, undeterred: "There is a brook a mile ahead. If we leave the horses there, they can survive a week or more. There will be little for them to eat and the water is sulfurous, but it will sustain them. We will cut across the hills to the north for three miles toward the cliff wall into which is carved the Stone Door."

I looked to Rodric, who shrugged. We seemed to have little choice in the matter. Without assistance, we would not find the way to Magas Komaron in time to warn Varastis. We allowed Ilona to lead us to the brook, which turned out to be dry. We carried only enough water to last the horses three more days; I had hoped to find water on the way to Magas Komaron. Barring that, one of us could climb one of the nearby peaks and fill the skins with melted snow. The horses would be unable to reach the snow on their own.

"They will die of thirst!" Vili cried.

"The brook is intermittent, as it is fed by a spring that erupts once a day. In a few hours, there will be water."

Vili was not mollified by her reassurances, but he did not object when I told him to unload the horses. Sensing that something was wrong, Ember neighed in protest, and I did my best to reassure her. We fed and watered them, leaving the feedbags open so they could eat the rest of the oats when they got hungry. I could only hope that Ilona was right about the brook. She unpacked her horse as well, taking only what supplies she could carry. If she were mistaken, her horse would face the same fate as ours.

The sun was hidden by the peak to our southwest, but long shadows told us that we had less than two hours before dark. If we hoped to find a stone door carved into a cliff wall before the morning, we would have to hurry. We followed Ilona as she scurried over the rocks on a meandering route that carried us slowly upward and toward the northeast. The scent of sulfur grew stronger as we traveled, until it at last became almost overpowering. As the sky began to darken overhead, we came to a canyon, at the bottom of which was a shallow pool of murky water. Steam roiled over the surface. Three rock formations, each some twenty feet tall, crouched like giants at the edges of the pool, roughly equidistant from each other.

"We must hurry," Ilona said. "We need to reach the northern mouth of the canyon. Oreg Huseges usually erupts just before dusk. When it does, this canyon will fill with boiling water. Even if we escape drowning, we will be badly scalded."

"Oreg Huseges is the spring that feeds the brook?" Vili asked.

"A geyser, yes. Pressure builds underground until it erupts from that crack yonder. First scalding steam and then hot water. Sometimes there is a warning. If you hear a whistle before we reach the crack, we are too late. Turn and run back the way we came."

"I will not speak for the others," I said, "but I will not turn back. If we do not reach the Stone Door today, we will be too late to warn Varastis."

"We are with you," Rodric said. "Onward."

Vili nodded and followed us as we began across the canyon floor. Ilona shook her head but followed as well.

The canyon was perhaps a quarter mile wide; the crack that Ilona had indicated zigzagged across the bottom of it. The crack was easily identifiable even in the dim light by the curtain of steam that wafted from it. The floor of the canyon was uneven; some places were dry while muddy pools persisted in others. The largest of these was the impression at the southern end of the canyon where the three rock formations perched.

I soon found my way blocked by a pool that looked to be several feet deep at the center; the steam that rolled across its surface suggested it would not be amenable to crossing.

"We must cross the chasm," Ilona panted from some distance behind me. "There."

I looked where she indicated and nodded. The crevice was perhaps ten feet across there. For most of its length it was thirty feet or more. I moved as quickly as I could over the uneven ground, skirting boulders and pools of foul water. I heard a faint whistle as I approached and did not slow, vaulting over the chasm in an easy leap. I stopped and awaited the others. Vili, who was the fastest runner among us, came next, besting my leaps by two feet despite his smaller size. Rodric reached the edge of the chasm and stopped. Ilona lagged some twenty paces behind. She was gasping and holding her side. The intensity of the whistling increased.

"Hurry, Rodric!" Vili cried, but his words were lost in the piercing scream from the canyon. Rodric went to Ilona and threw her arm around his neck. He helped her to the edge. I had little sympathy for this woman; it was one of her kind that had been responsible for my six-year stint in Nincs Varazslat. But without her, I doubted we would find the Stone Door in time. I watched, fists clenched at my sides, as Rodric pleaded with her to cross the chasm. She held her side and shook her head. Then she put her hand on his shoulder and spoke to him, pointing toward the northern end of the canyon. Was she telling him how to find the Stone Door? Or was this a trick of the sort for which the acolytes of Turelem were notorious?

Rodric shook his head. Blast him! I wanted to tell him to leave the woman and leap across: if she intended to trick us, it would be just as well that we left her, and if she were telling the truth, we did not need her. No harm would come to her if she ran back to the horses now. But my words would not reach him across the screeching chasm, and in any case it was clear that Rodric would not leave her. At last she appeared to agree to attempt the leap.

She and Rodric backed several steps away from the edge and he motioned toward her to go first. She took several deep breaths and then sprinted toward the chasm. Her leap would have cleared the chasm easily, but she slipped on loose gravel and came up short. She grasped futilely at the smooth rock on the other side and would have fallen into the chasm had Vili and I not each grabbed one of her wrists. We pulled her to safety just as a sheet of white steam blasted forth from the chasm. A moment later, Rodric burst through the curtain, crumpling to the ground a few feet away from us. His clothes were damp and a blanket of steam enveloped him. As soon as he caught his breath, he began to scream. The steam around him dissipated, and I saw that every inch of his skin was bright red.

Unthinking, I unstoppered my waterskin and doused his face and hands with it. Rodric continued to scream, and I snatched the waterskins Rodric and Ilona carried as well. When I'd spent our entire supply of water, Rodric's pain seem to ease a bit. His skin was still red, and I could see blisters beginning to appear on his wrists and cheeks.

"Konrad, we have to move!" cried Vili. I turned to see that the sheet of steam had turned into a wall of water. It was only a slight breeze carrying the water away from us that had spared the rest of us from being scalded. I helped Rodric to his feet and we ran toward the eastern wall of the canyon, where the ground was a bit higher. The scalding water was already filling the lower parts of the canyon.

"No!" Ilona shouted from behind. "If we go that way, we will be trapped. Follow the canyon wall north!"

I turned to Rodric, who was badly burned but seemed otherwise uninjured. He nodded. "Go!"

There was no time to argue. I turned north and ran along the gravel bed, parallel to the canyon, and the others followed. A few paces to our left was a wall of water and steam nearly a hundred feet high; even with the breeze carrying the mist away from us, the heat was nearly unbearable. As the canyon continued to flood, we found ourselves splashing through an inch of scalding water. The odor of sulfur was almost overpowering. I felt sorry for Ilona, who was bringing up the rear and must be getting the worst of the splashing. The oiled leather of my boots was waterproof, but scalding water splashed my trousers and had begun to work its way down my calves.

At last we reached the end of the water wall. More precisely, we reached a point where the wall gave way to a roiling bloom of water in the center of a shallow pool. The water at our feet was already two inches deep and getting deeper; my feet felt like they were on fire. The only escape was a slope of loose rock to our right that formed a ramp up to a narrow shelf along the eastern wall. To reach it, though, we would need to run another hundred paces through scalding hot water. The deeper impressions in the canyon had already been filled, and now the water level was rising even faster than before.

I had reached a patch of gravel that rose just above the water and stopped a moment for the others to catch up. Vili, whose ragged shoes were little defense against the scalding water, sprinted past me, his feet barely disturbing the surface. Rodric came up next to me, followed shortly by Ilona. I saw terror on Rodric's face. His burns must have hurt him terribly, and the idea of splashing through another hundred yards of scalding water must have horrified him. If he fell, he might not get up again. But there was no going back: the water was even deeper behind us.

"Rodric, we cannot stop," Ilona pleaded, seeing the look on Rodric's face as he surveyed the distance we still had to go to reach safety. Rodric glanced back to see a wave of water rushing toward us: having exhausted every pit and low-lying crevice, the flood had nowhere to go but across the canyon floor. Rodric groaned but stepped into the water again and ran toward the rock fall. I ran alongside him, hoping to catch him if he stumbled. Ilona, panting hard, managed to keep pace a short distance behind.

We weren't fast enough to outpace the wave, but it had dissipated somewhat by the time it reached us. Still, the shock of the heat on my calves nearly made me fall. Rodric cried out but did not stumble. Ahead of us, Vili had reached the rocks. Having climbed high enough to avoid the encroaching water, he fell to the ground and tore off his shoes. Rodric slipped as he climbed onto the gravel, but I grabbed his arm and helped him to safety. Ilona arrived a few seconds after us, just ahead of another wave that crashed against the rocks and splashed us with hot spray.

"Keep... moving," Ilona panted, crawling on her hands and knees up the slope of gravel. Rodric and I groaned in unison as we saw that we still were not safe: the water continued to rise rapidly and would soon reach us. We got to our feet and climbed up the slope to the shelf that ran along the eastern canyon wall. I could see from the erosion and striations of mineral deposits below us that the water did not ordinarily rise to this level. At last we were safe.

But still we could not rest: there was barely room to stand on the shelf, and we would have to hurry if we hoped to find the Stone Door before nightfall. Most of the canyon was already shrouded in darkness. We continued along the shelf for several minutes, the stink of sulfur growing gradually stronger until we came to an opening in the rock from which poured hot steam and foul-smelling vapor.

"Do not stop," Ilona said. "The path continues on the other side of the cave."

We did as she instructed, Rodric moaning as the steam touched his burns. We passed the cave opening quickly, but it was some time before we were free of the stench. Vili had to stop to retch, and I nearly did myself. I walked carefully along the path with my hand against the rock wall, dizzy from the noxious vapors. I was relieved when the narrow shelf abruptly widened into a broad plateau.

"This way," Ilona said, slipping past me and starting diagonally across the plateau. Rodric, Vili and I followed without a word. It was now dark as night in the canyon; overhead a deepening azure sky told us the sun had not yet set, but little light penetrated the canyon. To our right, the ominous black shadow of the eastern canyon wall towered over us. Ilona stopped abruptly and I nearly ran into her. We had reached the foot of the cliff.

It was a sheer stone wall, so uniform and featureless that it was essentially invisible in the dim light. Only the contrast with the gray-blue sky far above indicated that there was anything there at all.

"The door is around here somewhere," Ilona said. "Do you have a torch?"

Vili produced a torch and I managed to light it with my flint and steel. I lit another torch from it and then handed the first to Ilona, who began walking to the right along the stone wall. I lit a third torch and handed it to Vili. "Head left, in case she's gone the wrong direction." Vili nodded and set off.

While they searched for the door, I tended to Rodric's burns. Lacking cool water, there wasn't much I could do but lance the worst of the blisters and bandage the burns to protect the skin.

"You know I'm not one to complain," Rodric said, "but oh, how it burns! What I would give for a sip of wine...."

"Don't talk foolishness," I said. "You suffered worse wounds than this as a Scout."

"Then at least do something to distract me from the pain. Sing me a song. How does the rest of the song about Varastis go? The part about the Stone Door?"

I hadn't brought up the song again for fear that the vagueness of the later stanzas would only demoralize the party, but I saw no harm in singing them now. Perhaps Rodric could help me make sense of them. I sang:

Turelem's eyes watched the plain and the heath
and all of the gaps in Galibar's Teeth
so clever Varastis took the way underneath
to Magas Komaron

"Who is Galibar?" asked Rodric.

That part I knew, from reading one of General Janos's books on mythology. "A huge dragon who was said to be slain on the plain of Savlos thousands of years ago. I assume Galibar's teeth are the jagged peaks of the southern Kerepes mountains."

"A reasonable hypothesis. Then Varastis reached Magas Komaron through a tunnel under the mountains?"

"That would seem to be the implication."

"Very good. What is the rest?"

I continued:

The door that goes nowhere can still be a key
if opened when ogres are having their tea
and the throat choked with poison will soon breathe free
toward Magas Komaron

A wizard can't tell the wind not to blow
but there are places where not even the wind can go
and there in the dark the glimmer did show
of Magas Komaron

Whatever it is that Varastis knows
it led him to the place where the beacon now glows
and he gazes down upon his helpless foes
from Magas Komaron

Rodric frowned. "That's it?"

"As far as I can recall."

"Well, the 'door that goes nowhere' must be the Stone Door Ilona speaks of. But how can a door be a key?"

I was spared the need to confess my ignorance by a shout from Ilona.

"Can you get up?" I asked Rodric.

"Indeed," Rodric said. "If you have no more songs to sing, it is better that I am occupied in something. Sitting here I have nothing to do but focus on my pain."

I helped him to his feet. I was about to shout to Vili when I saw his torch moving toward us. Together, we followed the cliff wall until we reached Ilona. She stood before an elaborate carving in the rock face. To her left and right were fluted columns that supported a lintel. Recessed between the columns was a door that appeared to be constructed not of stone, but of plates of riveted steel. No hinges were evident, but on the right side of the door, about halfway up, was a handle in the form of a sort of recessed hand-crank.

"Can it be opened?" I asked.

"Be my guest," Ilona said, taking a step back.

"Douse all the torches but one," I said as I handed mine to Vili. "We may need them later." Vili and Rodric doused the torches while Ilona continued to hold hers, illuminating the door with a flickering yellow light.

I put my hand on the handle. It squeaked a bit but turned smoothly. At a quarter turn, there was a click and it stopped. I pulled on the handle and the door swung open. Its movement was completely silent but it provided more resistance than I expected. The resistance increased the more the door opened. Beyond it was a wall of blank stone.

"The door that goes nowhere," Rodric said.

I nodded, struggling to hold the door ajar. It was now almost perpendicular to the rock face, and I did not have the strength to pull it any farther. The door itself was nearly four inches thick and very heavy, but not heavy enough to account for the resistance. It was as if the door was connected to a massive spring; if I let it go, it would swing shut.

"This is as close to Magas Komaron as the acolytes have gotten," Ilona said. "Our cartographers have confirmed that if one could proceed through the door, she would be headed directly toward the beacon. But as you see, there is nothing beyond the door but solid rock."

"Vili, help me with this," I grunted. Vili scurried around Ilona and put himself behind the door. Together we opened it a few more inches. The resistance decreased suddenly at this point, and the door swung open a few degrees more on its own, nearly causing me to fall to the ground. I let go of the handle and the door remained open.

"Strange," Ilona said. "It ordinarily swings shut."

"The song says to open the door when the ogres are having their tea," I said.

"Song?" Ilona asked. "You mean the song you were singing to Rodric a moment ago?"

I ignored her. "A reference to the eruption of the geyser, no doubt," Rodric said. "The 'ogres' may be those rock formations we passed. The impression they lean toward would be filled with hot water shortly after an eruption."

Ilona frowned.

"Have the acolytes never attempted to open the door during an eruption?" I asked.

"It is dangerous to come here during an eruption, as you have seen," Ilona said. "Besides, it seems to have done you no good. The way is closed to you as it has been to us."

She was right about that: opening the door had not caused the stone wall to evaporate.

"According to the song," Rodric said, "Varastis took 'the way underneath.'"

"Underneath what?" Vili asked. "The mountains?"

"Presumably," I said. "But perhaps also underneath the door."

"Nonsense," Ilona said. "How can one go underneath the door?"

"The cave we passed," Rodric said. "The passage that spewed noxious vapors. It might pass directly underneath this point."

"It might very well," I said. "Quickly, while the door still stands open!" I turned and moved quickly across the plateau the way we had come. I seized the torch from Ilona and led the party back along the shelf to the cave. This time there was no stench of sulfur; in fact, cool air was being sucked into the passage.

"The door is a valve!" Rodric cried. "Somehow it redirects the flow of air!"

"How much longer will the eruption last?" I asked Ilona, as she approached the opening.

"Not long. A few minutes, perhaps."

"The valve is held open by the flow from the geyser," I said. "As long as it remains open, the passage is safe."

"What if we prop open the door?" Vili asked.

"I doubt it works that way," I said. I'd read something in one of General Janos's books about ancient machines powered by steam. "The door is a lever to open the valve, but the valve will close when the pressure dies, whether the door is open or not."

"Then we may only have a few minutes before the noxious vapors resume," Rodric said. "How do we know we can get through in time?"

"We don't," I said. "But we don't have time to wait for the next eruption. Those who still wish to seek Magas Komaron, Follow me!"

CHAPTER FIVE

I plunged into the cave, not waiting to see if the others followed. They knew the risks as well as I, and there was no time for a discussion on the matter. If we were to have any chance of beating Voros Korom to Magas Komaron, we would have to proceed while the geyser was still erupting. I just hoped that Rodric was right about the cave: if this were not the "way underneath"—or, for that matter, if this were all an elaborate joke perpetrated by Bolond—we would asphyxiate for nothing. Rodric groaned softly behind me; he was undoubtedly in great pain.

As I ventured further into the cave, though, I was somewhat encouraged: the floor was rough but fairly even, and the ceiling was high enough to allow me to pass without bending over. The cave seemed to be a natural vent that had been widened to allow people to pass through it. That implied there was something on the other side. Whether we would reach it before the noxious fumes and scalding vapor returned was another question. For now, the tunnel was filled with fresh, cool air being pulled from the outside. Besides the almost imperceptible whisper of air moving through the tunnel, the only sounds were footsteps: my own, as well as the footsteps of those foolhardy enough to follow me.

The one consolation was that there was no way to get lost: there was only one tunnel, which meandered through the mountain in what seemed to be a more-or-less easterly direction, descending as it went. Deeper and deeper we went into the mountain, until I was certain that if the flow of air shifted again, we would never make it to the surface in time. I did not attempt to keep track of the passage of time, but the geyser could not last much longer.

At last we came to a vast cavern, the bottom of which was shaped like a shallow bowl. A pool of still water occupied the lower half of the bowl. Sulfur hung in the atmosphere; the air from the surface had not completely expunged the foul vapor. On the opposite wall of the cavern was a dark opening that was presumably the continuation of the tunnel. If we were careful, we could make our way around the edge of the pool without falling in. Kneeling at the edge of the pool, I touched the water with my fingertips. It was warm, but not scalding. The others emerged from the tunnel behind me, and I saw that our party—including Ilona—was all there.

"The tunnel seems to continue that way," I said, pointing to the opening. "We must move quickly but be careful not to slip. If any of us falls into the pool, we may be unable to…" I trailed off, sensing that something had changed.

"The breeze has shifted," Ilona said, and I realized it was true: hot, damp air swept across my face. For now, it was only the fresh air that had filled the tunnel beyond, but soon the poisonous vapor would return. "It will take some time for it to fill this cavern," Ilona went on. "If we turn back now—"

"If you wish to turn back now, do so," I snapped. "I'll waste no more breath on the matter."

"We're with you, Konrad," Rodric said, his voice strained. "But how can we survive that noxious wind? If it doesn't boil us alive, we will surely succumb to the poison."

"What does the song say?" Vili asked.

Feeling a fool, I forced myself to recite the stanza:

A wizard can't tell the wind not to blow
but there are places where not even the wind can go
and there in the dark the glimmer did show
of Magas Komaron

"Where can the wind not go?" Rodric asked.

Rodric and Vili both looked to me for the answer. I felt that I should have been able to come up with it, but my mind was consumed by the dread of the poisonous wind, which would return at any moment.

"Underwater," Ilona said at last. As she said it, I knew she was right.

"A lot of good that does us," Rodric said. "Neither can we breathe underwater."

"Perhaps we don't need to," I said, and threw my torch into the water. The torch winked out and the cavern was plunged into darkness. The sickening odor of sulfur intensified, and I knew that the poisonous wind had reached the cavern. If I was wrong in my hunch, we would all soon be dead. I could only hope that we were overcome by the poison before the steam boiled the flesh from our bodies.

"There!" cried Vili. "Near the center of the pool!"

I saw it as well. Something glittered faintly in the water. Glittering meant light, and light meant another way out of the cave.

"Drop everything!" I ordered, unslinging my pack and stripping off my cloak. "Dive for that light!" There was no time to remove my boots, and I couldn't bear to leave my rapier. I took a deep breath, nearly choking on the sulfurous stench, and dived into the pool.

At first I could see nothing but the faint glitter at the bottom of the pool, but as I swam deeper, I caught sight of a distant opening in the rock ceiling through which a dim light poured. The glitter seemed to come from a mass of crystals that refracted the light from the shaft above. I pointed toward the shaft, but I doubted the others could see me in the near-total darkness. Lungs burning, I swam toward the light.

Reaching the opening of the shaft, I saw that it was barely large enough for a man to swim through. It led upwards at a diagonal toward the surface. I entered the shaft and swam perhaps twenty feet, at which point the shaft opened into a wide, shallow, pool. I burst above the surface, gasping for breath. Vili shot up next to me, followed shortly by Ilona and then Rodric. The air here was cool and fresh. On the distant horizon was the beacon of Magas Komaron, aligned perfectly with the shaft through which we'd just arrived. I shuddered to think what would have become of us if it had been a foggy night.

We swam to the edge of the pool and climbed onto the rocks. Once I'd made sure we'd all survived the ordeal and were in no immediate danger, I took a moment to get my bearings. To the west loomed the massive wall of granite through which we'd just come; to the east, the rocky ground sloped gradually down to a deep canyon. Farther to the east, perhaps ten miles distant, was a solitary peak that came to an unnaturally acute point. The beacon winked to us from the top.

"We camp here for the night," I said, and received no objections. We were all exhausted, and this would be treacherous ground to travel at night. I'd never been to this part of the mountains—until yesterday I'd thought it unreachable!—but Rodric and I had spent enough time in the Kerepes range to know that it was foolish to travel at night, even if you followed a known path. One wrong step and you'd tumble a quarter mile into a ravine and never be heard from again. Here we at least had water, and the ground radiated enough heat to make a fire unnecessary, even without our bedrolls and other supplies. Once I'd made the decision, fatigue came over me more quickly than the poisonous wind. I managed to strip off my boots but left my damp clothes on. I lay down on a bed of sand next to the pool and dreamt of Beata.

CHAPTER SIX

B y the time I awoke, the sun was already peeking over the mountains to the east. Rodric and Ilona sat talking on a boulder nearby, but Vili was nowhere to be seen. Rodric seemed to be feeling better; no doubt the cold air relieved some of the pain of his burns. I was about to reproach Rodric for letting me sleep so long when Vili returned with his shirt full of cranberries. We'd had nothing to eat since the previous afternoon and had left our provisions in the cave. Rodric and Vili confessed to having drunk some of the water from the pool before going to sleep, and they seemed to be no worse for it, so we sated our thirst and ate our fill of berries. Rodric seemed somewhat better than the previous night; the cold air was a relief for his burns. Our clothes were still damp and the rest of us were shivering, so we did not tarry. We filled the two skins that we still had with us and set off in the direction of Magas Komaron.

We followed a rough trail that snaked its way down the mountainside, reaching the floor of the canyon just after noon. The trail continued northwest alongside a shallow stream for two miles and then seemed to vanish; with some effort, we found a continuation of it on the other side of the stream. This led us gradually uphill for a few more miles, ending at the lip of the canyon. The foot of the mountain on which Magas Komaron perched was now less than three miles distant. The ground here was flat and spotted with clumps of grasses and scrub bushes; it was easy to traverse without a path.

I led the way, while Vili brought up the rear. Rodric and Ilona chatted like old friends, and I grew concerned that they were getting too close. The acolytes were sworn to eradicate sorcery, and we were leading her right to Varastis. Without his help, Nagyvaros would fall to Voros Korom, but without Ilona, we would not have made it this far. The conversation between Rodric and Ilona had been inconsequential so far; Rodric knew a great deal about the vegetation that grew in the mountains, and Ilona peppered him with endless questions every time we passed a new type of shrub or wildflower. At last, though, the conversation turned toward business, as I knew it must.

"Why do you seek Magas Komaron?" Ilona asked innocently.

"That question is better addressed to the leader of our party," Rodric replied.

"You do not have your own motivations?" Ilona asked, evidently not caring that I could hear her.

"Vili and I follow Konrad. If he seeks Magas Komaron, we seek it as well."

Vili grunted his assent from the rear.

"It is as simple as that?"

"Aye."

"At some point I shall inquire what inspires such unquestioning loyalty," Ilona said. "But for now I will have to be content to pose the question to the one you call your leader. What of it, Konrad? Why do you seek Magas Komaron?"

"I owe you no explanation."

"Certainly not, but if we are to go to Magas Komaron together, it might be wise to be clear on one another's motivations."

"I'm quite aware of the acolytes' motivations in seeking Magas Komaron."

"Are you?"

"You wish to find the way to the sorcerers' sanctuary so that you can finish the task of eradicating them."

"An oversimplification, to be sure, but you are correct that the acolytes wish to arrest the dissemination of forbidden knowledge of the arcane. Knowing so much of my kind, however, you have me at a disadvantage. Tell me at least: are you a friend of Varastis or a foe?"

"I do not know the man."

"But you go to seek his help."

I sighed. The truth was that I envied Ilona her clarity of purpose. Why *was* I going to Magas Komaron? To save Nagyvaros or to avoid being doomed to an eternity serving Szarvas Gyerek in Veszedelem? Or was I simply fueled by a desire to learn more about Eben so that I could have my revenge on him? If I succeeded in defeating Voros Korom, was I doing the work of my enemy? Ilona was untroubled by such questions. To the acolytes, sorcery was evil and needed to be wiped out. That was the end of it. I decided it would do no harm to give her some sense of the true complexity of the situation.

"The man who murdered the woman I loved has sent a demon and his horde of wraiths to Magas Komaron to kill Varastis and his followers so that Varastis cannot thwart the demon's efforts to lay waste to Nagyvaros. I am hoping to reach Magas Komaron ahead of the demon to warn Varastis and ally with him against the demon. Even if I reach Magas Komaron in time, the warning will probably do no good, and if by some miracle we succeed in vanquishing the horde, I will in all likelihood be doing the bidding of the man I once swore to kill, but who still torments me from a shadow world beyond life and death. I trust this answers your question."

We did not speak of the matter again.

The mountain was a near perfect cone, rising some three thousand feet above the plateau on which we stood. We reached its foot by late afternoon. The sides were sheer rock, so steep as to be nearly impossible to scale, but we saw as we approached that a stairway had been carved into the face. It looped around the base of the mountain to the left, spiraling twice before disappearing again on the far side. There could be no doubt from this distance that Magas Komaron was no mere pinnacle of rock left behind by some chance fissure: parapets and crenelated towers could now be seen.

There seemed to be no way up but the staircase, so we made our way toward it. We made no effort at stealth; undoubtedly we'd been seen from miles away. With even a minimal force defending Magas Komaron, it would be virtually impregnable to any ordinary attack. I wondered, as I began the climb up that long stone staircase, how long it would stand against Voros Korom and his spectral horde.

Somewhat to my surprise, Ilona proceeded up the staircase after me with no comment or protest. I had half-expected her to bolt once the way to Magas Komaron was clear, as her intention was presumably to deliver this information to Delivaros, not to confront Varastis on her own. But evidently either curiosity had gotten the better of her or I was mistaken about her mission.

It took us nearly two hours to reach the eastern side of the mountain. The view was much like that from the western side: the mountain on which Magas Komaron perched arose from a plateau roughly in the center of the range. Beyond the peaks to the west lay the plains of the Barbaroki. The sun was already low in the sky, illuminating the rock face with an orange glow. We rounded the northern side of the mountain with only the dim light of dusk to guide us and then plunged into darkness as we rounded a corner back toward the side facing west. A cold western wind had picked up, and we were grateful to be in the lee of the mountain. We'd lost our torches in the cave, but the stone steps were so precisely hewn that by keeping one hand on the rock wall to our left we had little trouble making our way in the near-total darkness. I marveled at the symmetry of the mountain itself; it was as if it had been formed with the idea of Magas Komaron in mind. I reflected, with a chill, that perhaps it had.

As we rounded the south side of the mountain again, the wind tore at our clothes and threatened to hurl us off the staircase. Thunder rumbled in the distance, and the clouds to the west flickered with lightning. We kept on, pressing our bodies flat against the rock face. At last we came again to the east side, and while the wind continued to buffet and howl, the gusts only pushed us against the mountain. So intent was I on fighting the wind's attempts to bash my head against the rock that when the wall abruptly ended, I nearly fell.

I found myself in a broad, flat courtyard surrounded by a low stone wall. In the near-darkness, I could just make out the silhouettes of several trees, as well as shrubs and beds of various other plants. The courtyard was a rough semicircle that seemed to take up half of the summit of the curiously conical mountain. The other half was dominated by the foreboding silhouette of a great castle, its spires and crenels making a jagged black line against a canopy of stars: Magas Komaron. In the highest tower blazed the beacon that had so befuddled travelers through these mountains.

The rest of the party came up alongside me. None of us spoke; we were numb with cold and exhaustion. Drops of rain began to pelt us. There was nothing to do but continue to the castle. I led the way across the courtyard to the massive door. Feeling a fool, I lifted my hand to knock, but the door began to open on its own. I put my hand on my rapier. The door creaked slowly inward and then stopped, leaving an opening just large enough for a man to slip through. I glanced back at Rodric, who nodded. I drew my rapier and went inside. The others followed, and we found ourselves in another, smaller, courtyard, within the castle walls. At first it seemed we were alone, but shortly I saw the glow of a lantern moving toward us across the courtyard. The lantern's flame flickered against the wind, and the rain began to fall in earnest. A man, hunched over and wearing a hooded cloak, approached. He stopped a few paces in front of us, holding up the lantern to examine our faces.

"Have you come to murder me?" he asked.

"No," I said.

"What about this one?" he asked, waving the lantern toward Ilona.

"I mean you no harm," Ilona said. "Are you Varastis?"

The man chuckled bitterly. "I am Domokos. You seek Varastis?"

"Yes," I said. "On a matter of great urgency. Are you one of his followers?"

Domokos nodded. "I will take you to him." Having evidently decided we were not a threat, the man turned and walked back the way he had come. Anxious to get out of the rain and wind, we followed.

We went into the castle, down a dark hallway, and down a steep flight of stone stairs. The howl of the wind diminished as we descended. After passing several storerooms, we came to a vast room lined with catacombs. Many of the catacombs were still open (and unoccupied), but several scores of them had been sealed with the rock-hard aggregate material used by the Builders. Farther in were a dozen that appeared to have been sealed more recently, with brick and mortar. Domokos led us to these.

"This one is Varastis, as you can see," he said, holding the lantern up to a crudely carved wooden plaques. "His followers sleep nearby. Except for me, of course. I was left alive to continue the important work of maintaining a sanctuary where no one is actually safe. If you've seen enough, I can take you back upstairs. I can't promise it's much more comfortable than this crypt, but there is soup and ale."

Thunder rumbled outside. I stared at the plaques. On them were written the names of thirteen men who represented my only hope to stop Voros Korom. Ilona came up beside me and put her hand on the plaque that read Varastis, feeling the grooves with her fingers. If she was pleased to see that Varastis and his followers were dead, she did not look it.

"They are all dead?" Rodric asked.

"I haven't checked recently," said Domokos, "but they were when I put them in there."

"What happened?" Ilona asked.

"You are an acolyte of Turelem?"

"I am."

"Then what happened is that someone did your work for you."

"The acolytes don't murder—"

"You are welcome to take shelter here for the night," Domokos snapped, "but please do not attempt to educate me regarding what the acolytes do and don't do. I fled my home to escape the wrath of the Cult of Turelem before you were born." Regaining his equanimity, he said, "This way, please."

He led us back upstairs to a dining hall that was dominated by a long oak table flanked by benches. The rain was now coming down in torrents, and the distant rumble of thunder had given way to deafening booms. Domokos doused the lantern as we entered, so the only light—other than flashes of lightning from under the door of the windowless room—came from a fire that blazed in a massive stone fireplace at the far end of the room. The air smelled of garlic and onions.

"You'll have to make do with everything soup," Domokos said, walking to a pot hanging over the fire. He threw back his hood to reveal a bald head and a thick gray beard. The dim, flickering light made it difficult to discern his age; one moment he seemed a young man, prematurely gray, and the next he seemed ancient. He took a ladle from a hook and began scooping stew into a large ceramic bowl. "Everything goes in the soup. Mostly onions and leeks, I'm afraid, but there is a little chicken. Salt is in short supply, so you may find it bland."

We had formed a semicircle around the fireplace, drawn by the heat and the scent of the stew. Domokos handed me the bowl and stood watching expectantly. There seemed to be no other bowls and no spoons. I thanked him and handed the bowl to Ilona, prompted by equal parts caution and chivalry. She accepted it suspiciously. Thunder boomed outside so loudly that I thought the castle itself must have been struck by lightning.

"What is your name?" Domokos said, turning to me.

"I am Konrad," I said.

"You bear the brand of a warlock," Domokos said, "but you travel with an acolyte?"

"I had little choice. Without her, we could not have found the way in time."

"You are a sorcerer?"

"No. I was given this brand against my will."

Domokos made no discernible reaction. "And these others?"

"Rodric and Vili. They are my companions and friends. What happened to Varastis and the others?"

Domokos motioned to the table. "Come, let us sit."

We went to the table and sat. Vili and Ilona took the two seats closest to the fire. Rodric sat to Ilona's left; Domokos sat between me and Vili. Ilona had tried the stew and apparently not found it objectionable; she passed the bowl to Vili.

"Why do you seek Varastis?" Domokos asked.

"I had wished to warn him. And to get his help."

"Warn him of what?"

"Voros Korom is on his way to Magas Komaron. He will likely attack tomorrow, during the full moon."

"Voros Korom! The demon still wanders the mountains of Veszedelem."

"You are mistaken. A sorcerer named Radovan brought him to our world."

Domokos frowned, evidently recognizing the name. "What of Radovan?"

"Radovan is dead."

"You are certain of this?"

"I claim to be certain of very little anymore, but I left him bleeding to death below the ruins of Romok. It was his blood that brought forth Voros Korom."

"Why would Voros Korom come here rather than seek his birthright in Nagyvaros?"

"He was persuaded by another sorcerer, a man named Eben, that only Varastis could prevent him from conquering Nagyvaros."

"Then Eben still lives?"

"He is exiled to the shadow world. The place called Veszedelem."

"It was he who gave you the brand?"

"Yes."

"But you are not a sorcerer. Why would he give up his power in that way?"

I was obliged to tell my story once again, starting with how I'd run into Eben at the Lazy Crow and ending with Voros Korom turning away from Nagyvaros toward Magas Komaron. Domokos seemed relieved to hear that I had allied with Eben only out of necessity.

"A clever trick, that," Domokos said. His demeanor had softened. "Sending the demon and his horde to Magas Komaron. Not that it will do any good."

"Do you think Eben knew Varastis was dead?"

Domokos shook his head. "I do not know. He may have assumed, as do most, that the beacon signifies that Varastis still lives."

"What happened to them? Varastis and his followers."

"Before I tell you how Varastis and the others were killed," Domokos said, "I should like to know what business the acolyte has here."

Ilona, who had been strangely silent since we left the catacombs, started. "I... I was given a message to deliver to Varastis."

"I am the closest thing Varastis has to a successor," Domokos said. "You can give the message to me."

Ilona shook her head. "If Varastis is dead, the matter is of little importance."

"Then you will return to Delivaros tomorrow?"

"I... do not know. I had not expected to be allowed to leave at all."

Domokos shrugged. "When I saw your party coming across the plain, I knew that you were either my salvation or my doom. Perhaps you are both. I decided at that moment that this was the last night the beacon would burn. I have spent seven years here alone. I consider my debt to Varastis paid. If I survive the full moon, I will leave this place."

"And go where?" I asked.

Domokos smiled. "That I will not tell you, in case the acolyte returns to report to her superiors."

"Then tell us of Varastis."

Domokos nodded. "Varastis and his followers were killed seven years ago by a man I had never seen before, and whom I've not seen since. The moon was full, as it will be tomorrow night. The stranger commanded a horde of spidery creatures the size of dogs that moved like shadows along the ground. All of our defenses were for naught. The shadow spiders slipped under the door and let the man in. Half of our number were dead before we even knew we were under attack. We'd become complacent, trusting in the inaccessibility of Magas Komaron to protect us, although I'm not certain what difference it would have made had we been on guard.

"I was with Varastis in a room overlooking the inner courtyard when we heard the screams. When Varastis saw the man in the courtyard, he seized me by the shoulders and said, 'Domokos, whatever happens, do not let the beacon die.' Before I could say a word, he had fled the room to face the intruder.

"Varastis and a few of the others seemed to understand what the shadow spiders were and were able to ward them off for a time, but they just kept coming. I survived only by luck: not knowing what else to do, I fled to the eastern tower. One of the creatures eventually found me, but as it was about to envelop me, sucking my life out as I had seen the things do to several of my comrades, the first rays of dawn peeked over the horizon. The light seemed to weaken the thing, and I managed to catch hold of one of its legs and hurl it from the tower. It dissipated in the shadows below.

"Ashamed of my cowardice, I ran back down the stairs to see if there was something I could do to aid Varastis and the others, but it was too late: all were dead, save Varastis himself, who was in the clutches of one of the spider-things. It pinned him to the ground, its tentacle-like legs wrapped around his body. Keeping myself hidden, I watched in horror as the unknown sorcerer approached Varastis. There was a brief exchange of words between the two, but I could not make out what was said. The man looked up, and for a moment I thought he had seen me, but he was only looking at the lightening sky. Realizing the shadow-spiders were weakening, he made a gesture with his hand and the one that had been holding Varastis suddenly released him. Before Varastis could react, one of the creature's legs had slipped into his mouth. Then another, and another. Before I could even gasp in horror, the thing had folded up on itself and begun to slide into Varastis's body. A second later, it had disappeared completely.

"I watched Varastis's body get up, but Varastis no longer controlled it. I will never forget the look of terror on his face as he lurched toward the gate, fighting the creature's hold on him with all his strength. The sorcerer followed him out, and I skulked along behind. I reached the gate just in time to see Varastis hurl himself off the mountain.

"That was the end of it. The spider-things faded and then disappeared, as shadows do. The sorcerer started back down the stairs, without even a glance back. I considered creeping up behind him to push him off the mountain, but I was haunted by Varastis's last words to me. *Whatever happens, do not let the beacon die.*

At that moment, it occurred to me that perhaps this was the reason I had been spared. Someone needed to make sure the beacon kept burning. I had just seen the sorcerer murder twelve men; surely he would not be so foolish as to allow me simply to push him off the stairs. It must be a trick! By the time I regained my nerve, the man was gone. I ran after him, but when I reached the place where the steps can be seen for nearly a mile, I saw nothing. It was as if he'd jumped off the edge of his own volition, or simply vanished. I returned to the castle and spent the next three days disposing of the dead.

"I have kept the beacon burning every night since then, for all the good it has done. For the first few nights, I was certain that the murderer, alerted by the beacon that his work was not finished, would return to kill me as well. Many times since then I wished he had. I wonder if I am truly doing the bidding of Varastis, or of the mysterious sorcerer who wishes the beacon to remain lit. Sometimes at night I think I hear him singing, but it is only the wind."

"Singing?" I asked.

Domokos nodded. "As he walked away, I heard him singing. I could not make out the words, but I remember the tune. A simple melody, like a child's song." He hummed a bit of the tune. I suppressed a shudder: I was certain it was one of Bolond's songs.

It could not be a coincidence: the man who had led me here was the same man who had murdered Varastis and his followers. Had Bolond brought me here only to kill me? The idea seemed far-fetched. Surely, if Bolond still lived and he wished to kill me, there were easier ways. In any case, he would have to hurry if he wished to kill me before Voros Korom did.

"Do you know the name Bolond?" I asked.

"Of course," Domokos said. It was he who first opened the gateway to Veszedelem, over a thousand years ago."

"Is it possible Bolond is still alive?"

"It is unlikely, but with sorcerers one never knows for certain. Bolond was said to have sought the gift of immortality. Why do you inquire about Bolond?"

I decided I had little choice but to trust Domokos. If he could not be trusted, we were already dead. "I believe it was

Bolond who sent me here," I said. "That is, he told me the way. Whether he actually intended for me to come here I cannot say. I am still not certain whether he was—or is—insane." I told Domokos of the singing I'd overhead in Nincs Varazslat and how one of the songs I'd inadvertently memorized had guided us here. "When you spoke of the murderer singing as he left, I couldn't help but wonder if it was the same man."

Domokos nodded thoughtfully. "It is a strange coincidence indeed. But if it truly was Bolond who came to you in the dungeon—and if it was also he who killed Varastis—then we have an even greater enemy than Voros Korom. One who is evidently immortal, at that."

"It does no good to worry about Bolond," I said. "He is either insane, in which case his actions are impossible to predict, or he is manipulating us toward some end that is beyond our comprehension. We have little choice but to face the more immediate threat. What do you know of Voros Korom? You spoke earlier of his 'birthright.' What did you mean? Why does he wish the destruction of Nagyvaros?"

"You must understand," said Domokos, "that even when Varastis was alive, I was not one of his inner circle of confidants. I was a middling practitioner of arcane arts who had the good fortune to learn of Varastis's midnight flight to Magas Komaron before your companion's kind could lay their hands on me. I learned a great deal from Varastis and the others, but it was quite clear that Varastis was very guarded in his dissemination of knowledge. Even those closest to him complained that he kept the greatest secrets to himself. It was, in fact, this very reticence that prompted Radovan to leave Magas Komaron."

"Eben mentioned that Radovan was one of Varastis's students."

"Early on, yes. But I'm getting ahead of myself. The point, in any case, is that there is much I do not know about Bolond and Voros Korom, but I will tell you what I can."

CHAPTER SEVEN

"I do not know where Bolond came from or how he learned to channel arcane energies. What I do know is that more than a thousand years ago, Bolond opened a gateway between our world and a place called Veszedelem, sometimes called the shadow world.

"It is said that Veszedelem was once a pleasant and prosperous world, but something happened to drain it of its vitality. If you have been to Veszedelem, you understand. It is a cold, dark place where the very substance of reality seems frayed and tattered. Bolond gathered together a group of wise men to determine what had gone wrong. These men knew that all of reality was held together by an element they called tvari. Their intent was to determine why Veszedelem was bleeding tvari, and to staunch the flow.

"The degradation of that world had caused horrible aberrations of humanity to arise, creatures that we would call monsters or demons. The most terrible of these was Arnyek, who plotted to end the suffering of Veszedelem by destroying it. To defend themselves against Arnyek's hordes, the sorcerers built a great keep, called Sotetseg. Sotetseg was designed to be accessible only by those whose blood was infused with tvari, but the sorcerers were too few to defend it from Arnyek. Many other demon lords had arisen to challenge Arnyek, and a few of these were recruited to work inside Sotetseg. These demons were bound by accords that prevented them from harming the sorcerers or interfering with their work.

"Sotetseg was built to attract and focus tvari, so the degradation that affected Veszedelem was minimized in its vicinity. The keep thus became a rallying point for human beings who still inhabited Veszedelem. Thousands of people settled on the plain nearby, taking refuge in the keep whenever the monsters came down from the mountains.

"For many years, Bolond and his sorcerers toiled in Sotetseg, trying to find a cure for the ailment that afflicted Veszedelem. Outside, Arnyek raised an army of monsters to wipe out humanity and destroy the keep. Sotetseg was by this time protected by powerful enchantments and might have stood against Arnyek's hordes forever were it not for a sorcerer named Lorenz. Lorenz had become convinced that the efforts to save Veszedelem were hopeless, and he betrayed the sorcerers to Arnyek, arranging for the gate to be left open so that Arnyek's assassins could get inside.

"Several of the sorcerers were killed, but Bolond succeeded in rallying the demons sworn to defend the keep, and the attackers were driven out. The defenders once again had control of the keep, but their project was in ruins. The library and laboratories had been burned, and only three of the sorcerers, along with Bolond, remained alive. Their task had always been daunting, and now it seemed impossible. The sorcerers lost faith in Bolond and they sealed themselves in the upper levels of a tower where he could not reach them.

"Realizing his project was a failure, Bolond decided to devote his efforts to saving the few human beings left alive on Veszedelem. The forces of Arnyek continued to grow, and it was clear he would soon turn his attention to the villages on the plain in order to stamp out the last vestige of humanity. Bolond's inquiries into the nature of tvari had revealed that Veszedelem was only one of many worlds, and he learned to harness tvari to travel between them. He traveled from world to world, looking for a safe place for the people to settle. He finally chose Orszag, in our world.

"At this time, the Plain of Savlos was mostly unpopulated, so he thought it safe to lead the refugees there. Those who have not trained their bodies to channel tvari cannot travel from world to world the way sorcerers do, so Bolond needed to build a gateway through which the refugees could travel to the new world. The gateway would be in the form of a temple constructed of massive stone slabs. While looking for a site for the temple, Bolond came across a tiny settlement called Telepules, just south of the current location of Nagyvaros.

"Telepules, presided over by a woman named Turelem, had been founded by a puritan group whose members had been persecuted in their homeland. Bolond met with Turelem, explaining his intention to build a temple to act as a permanent gateway between the two worlds. Seeing that the tranquility of Telepules would be disturbed by the gateway, Turelem refused his request. But Bolond appealed to the people of Telepules, persuading them that their lives would be improved by the union of the two worlds. Many of the people were already dissatisfied with Turelem's rule, and Bolond made a persuasive case. Turelem was thrown into the river Zold and apparently killed. With the help of the locals, Bolond built the temple at the current site of Nagyvaros.

"But as the refugees began to pour through from Veszedelem, Bolond realized there was another problem: for those who had been born in the corrupted world of Veszedelem, our world had too much vitality, too much tvari. The sun blinded them, the odors of flowers nauseated them, the blandest of foods burned their tongues. Many came anyway to escape certain death at the hands of Arnyek, but they suffered greatly.

"Bolond solved this problem too, after a fashion: because of his ousting of Turelem and his displays of arcane power, the locals now considered him a prophet, if not a god. He capitalized on this by urging them to build a great temple of his design from rock slabs taken from the Soveny Mountains. In reality, the temple was designed to absorb tvari, to make the area around Telepules a bit more like the shadow world the refugees had left—not enough to cause the horrible aberrations of that place, but enough to allow the people from Veszedelem to live in relative comfort.

"The end result, though, made no one happy: the discomfort of the refugees, while ameliorated to some degree, was not eliminated. Some burrowed underground to avoid the glare of the sunlight and the smell of vegetation. They ate the blandest of gruels, sometimes mixed with chalk or sand to kill the taste. And as refugees continued to arrive, fights broke out for control of the land nearest the temple. A curious social structure developed, with the upper castes building homes next to—and under—the temple. People tunneled far underground and built massive towers in order to create more living space near the temple. These people are now called the Builders, and the strange city they built was called Elhalad.

"The locals quickly realized they'd been deceived. The temple they had toiled to build to bring the favor of the gods had turned the area into a strange, dismal place inhabited by pale beings who lived like worms underground and built ugly stone towers that loomed over the plain like the spines of some huge reptile. But the locals were vastly outnumbered by the newcomers, and they could do little but build new settlements out of reach of the blight. Bolond had hoped the refugees would mix with the locals and eventually produce offspring better suited to life in our world, but instead the two groups became completely isolated and grew to hate each other.

"Bolond feared that the locals would appeal for help to one of the four kingdoms that bordered the plain, leading to the overthrow of Elhalad and the extermination of the newcomers. Each of these kingdoms existed in a state of antipathy with the others, and Bolond determined to take advantage of this. He traveled to one of the kingdoms and met with its king, proposing an alliance against the other kingdoms. The alliance was cemented by the marriage of the king's daughter to a man from Veszedelem, whom Bolond had set up as 'king' at Elhalad. The product of this strange union was an abomination. They called him Voros Korom.

"It was clear from the beginning that Voros Korom was no ordinary child. His appearance was ordinary enough—when he appeared at all. Voros Korom sometimes seemed to flicker in and out of existence, occasionally disappearing altogether only to reappear a few seconds later, sometimes several feet away. Then Voros Korom began to grow.

"By the age of three, Voros Korom was as tall as a full-grown man. After the child inadvertently crushed the skull of his nurse, he was placed under constant watch by men in full armor. When he was five, he killed three of these men with his bare hands. After that, Voros Korom was left alone to do as he pleased. By the age of ten, he towered over the tallest men in Elhalad. He could break a man's thigh with one hand. He killed frequently, though generally without malice. He walked the streets of Elhalad, eating and drinking as he pleased, leaving a wake of destruction. And someday he would be King of Elhalad.

"Many people, both in Elhalad and in the kingdoms surrounding the plain, feared this eventuality, and one man arose to take advantage of this fear: a sorcerer named Eben.

"Eben's origin is nearly as mysterious as Bolond's. What is known is that he conspired with Elhalad's enemies against the city and used his magic to conceal their armies as they marched across the plain. Soldiers poured through the streets, murdering most of the inhabitants, who were loath to leave the city. The defenders were few and weak, although Voros Korom alone killed nearly three hundred of the attackers before finally falling in a rain of arrows. Realizing he was defeated, he disappeared, retreating to Veszedelem. Bolond was forced to flee as well; as far as I know, he has not been heard from since. Eben is said to be able to transfer his soul from one body to another, and in this way has achieved a sort of immortality. At the time of Varastis's death, he believed Eben was still alive and waiting for the right time to work his own designs on Nagyvaros.

"The invaders tore down the gateway to Veszedelem and the temple and dragged the stone slabs to the Maganyos Valley. Several hundred of the city's residents, desperate to escape, attempted to flee through the gate back to Veszedelem. Some made it, but many more were trapped between worlds as the gateway was torn down. These became the wraiths that now haunt the valley.

"Although the temple had been torn down, the blight remained at the ruins of Elhalad. It became known as a cursed place and remained uninhabited for nearly six hundred years. Eventually, the Szaszok people began to build settlements on the plain. By this time, the war had been almost entirely forgotten, except for fragmentary oral accounts. The blight had faded. Those who came to the ruins of Elhalad now found it pleasant and hospitable. Some settlers moved into the ruins and others built dwellings around or on top of them. Slowly the city we know as Nagyvaros came into being.

"As Nagyvaros grew, so did the cult of Turelem, centered at Delivaros. I will not bore you with the details of how that detestable cult came into being; I trust you are sufficiently familiar with its history for our purposes. For most of the history of Nagyvaros, sorcery was not illegal, but knowledge of the arcane was tightly controlled. Hidden in the tunnels left behind by the Builders were numerous books and artifacts hinting at the existence of Veszedelem and the power of tvari. Agents of the Governor scoured the tunnels looking for such items, which—due to the wealth and influence of Delivaros—invariably ended up in the hands of the acolytes.

"Then, nearly thirty years ago, a young man in the employ of the Governor's office came across something in the tunnels of Nagyvaros that allowed him to tap into the power of the shadow world. His name was Varastis. One of Varastis's earliest students was a man named Radovan. I was one of the last.

"The acolytes put pressure on the city-states to outlaw sorcery and capture the sorcerers. Varastis was aware of the danger and had long planned to flee with his students to Magas Komaron, but he was betrayed by Radovan, who led the acolytes, abetted by agents of the Governor, to the school. Only Varastis and twelve of his students escaped.

"Radovan spent many years working in secret, trying to learn what Varastis had kept secret from him, but he was thwarted in his efforts to explore the tunnels below Nagyvaros by the acolytes. The last I heard, he had taken a job working for the Arcanist's office, but that was over ten years ago. News reaches Magas Komaron rarely if at all."

"Radovan became the Chief Arcanist," I said. "Evidently what he learned in that position convinced him of the need to summon Voros Korom."

Domokos nodded. "He wanted unrestricted access to the tunnels. Even as Chief Arcanist, he would be closely watched by the acolytes. There are places below Nagyvaros that the Governor himself cannot go. If Voros Korom destroyed the city, no one could stop him from seeking whatever it is he hoped to find below it."

"But now Radovan is dead, and Voros Korom is off his leash."

"Thanks to you, evidently."

"And Eben," I said.

"Yes. Strange that he resurfaced after so much time. I suppose I never really believed he was still alive. Nor Bolond, for that matter. For some time I entertained the notion that I was the only sorcerer still living."

"Eben seems to have been hiding out in Nagyvaros, right under Radovan's nose. He had a vast secret lair inside the Hidden Quarter. Although if his goal was to remain unnoticed, taking on this brand was a strange choice."

"The brand greatly enhances a sorcerer's power. Perhaps he performed the ritual to defeat Radovan, or perhaps it was necessary for his own plans. I'm afraid I don't know enough, either of the nature of the brand, or of Eben's plans, to say."

"There is something I don't understand," Rodric interjected. "Eben said that Voros Korom was intent on destroying Nagyvaros, yes? But if he considers himself the rightful ruler of the city, why would he destroy it? What good does it do him to rule over a pile of ruins and corpses?"

Domokos shook his head. "Perhaps he is motivated only by revenge. I cannot think of any other reason Radovan would have summoned him."

"Radovan's motives and those of Voros Korom may differ," I said. "Is the demon still bound by Radovan's commands, even though Radovan is dead?"

"That depends on the agreement they made," said Domokos, "and whether Voros Korom intends to honor it. He is not bound by the ancient accords the way the demons of Sotetseg are. Even if Radovan lived, his control over Voros Korom would have been limited. If he intended to use Voros Korom against Nagyvaros, it is because he knew Voros Korom would lay waste to the city if given the chance."

"There is another complication," I said. "Radovan intended to use my blood to summon Voros Korom. He was going to add some of his own blood to mine and then kill me, so that control over Voros Korom would default to him. Instead, the reverse happened: Radovan supplied most of the blood, with a little of mine mixed in."

"Then it is possible that *you* can command Voros Korom?" Rodric asked.

I shrugged. Domokos seemed no more certain than I. "I'm afraid the question goes beyond my ken," he said. "A battle between a sorcerer and a demon often comes down to a question of will. If you were to meet Voros Korom on the plain without fear and command him to return to Veszedelem, he might comply. On the other hand, he might tear you to pieces without a thought. I simply don't know. I have some limited ability to manipulate arcane energy, but my knowledge of Veszedelem and the creatures that inhabit that world is second-hand. I have never been there. Very few have the ability to travel from one world to another."

My heart sank. Could it be that our only hope in helping us defeat Voros Korom knew less of the shadow world than I did? So far, nothing he had told us would help us in the slightest.

"What other alternatives do we have?" Rodric asked. "Is it even possible to fight him?"

Domokos nodded. "Voros Korom is a creature of flesh and blood. He is formidable, but he can be wounded and even killed. He can move between our world and Veszedelem at will, but he must be present in our world to affect it."

"In other words," Rodric said, "he is vulnerable when he attacks."

"Precisely. Also, the wraiths weaken if he does not remain poised between the two worlds. He can neither exert his full strength nor fully retreat without the wraiths' power diminishing. And it is the wraiths that are the true threat."

"Is it true," ventured Vili quietly, "that they absorb the souls of their victims?"

"It is," Domokos said. "My understanding is that each wraith is in fact a collective of many souls trapped in between our world and Veszedelem. Each of these souls is constantly struggling to escape this in-between state, and they are drawn to the souls of living beings in our world. They move like the wind, and their touch is deadly. The victim's soul is added to the collective, but the collective's thirst is not abated."

Vili nodded, swallowing hard, but said nothing. Eben had told me all this already, but I had seen no point in burdening Vili or the others with the information.

"Do the wraiths have any weaknesses?" I asked.

"Only one: they are dependent for their existence on Voros Korom. If he dies, they will dissipate. They cannot survive without him as a link between our worlds."

"Might they simply return to the ruins of Romok?" I asked.

"It is too far. If Voros Korom were to die here, the wraiths would die as well."

"And they would truly die?" Vili asked. "All of the souls they have captured will be at peace?"

"They would know the same peace that is granted to all dead men," Domokos said. He gave Vili a curious look.

Vili nodded but again did not elaborate. I did not feel it was my place to explain Vili's interest in the wraiths, and Rodric followed my lead. Having eaten our fill of the soup, I'd begun to feel the full extent of my exhaustion. The others looked nearly as tired as I.

"There are plenty of beds," Domokos said, seeming to read my thoughts. "I will keep watch until the moon is past its zenith, but it is unlikely Voros Korom will come before tomorrow night. You may as well sleep while you can." Rodric and Vili nodded tiredly; Ilona seemed to be lost in thought. "Konrad, you look like you are ready to pass out on the table. If the others don't mind, I will show you to your room first."

I glanced at Rodric, who nodded. He had evidently come to the same conclusion as I: we had no choice but to trust Domokos. If he intended to murder us in our sleep, we might as well get it over with. Domokos got up from the table and re-lit the lantern. I followed him out of the room.

We went down a long, narrow stone passageway and stopped at a door. He opened it to reveal a small, modestly appointed bedroom. The sight of an actual bed nearly brought me to tears.

Domokos asked if I would like him to light the candle that rested on a small table near the bed, but I shook my head. I slumped onto the bed, barely able to keep my eyes open.

"Good," he said. "I know what you must do, but you should sleep first. You will need your strength. He may be the only ally we have, but he is not to be trusted."

I nodded. Domokos bid me goodnight and left the room, closing the door behind him. I took off my boots and lay down. Domokos was right: Eben was not to be trusted. On the other hand, I had no firm reason to believe Domokos could be trusted either. I wondered if he had urged me not to go to Veszedelem tonight so that Eben could not warn me of some threat. Should I have told Eben I planned to go to Magas Komaron? Who was the greater danger? Eben or Domokos? And how did Bolond, who seemed to have manipulated me into coming here, fit into all of this? Not knowing whom to trust was exhausting.

I closed my eyes and fell asleep.

CHAPTER EIGHT

I slept until mid-morning. Sunlight filtered through slats in a small window over my bed. The rain had stopped during the night, but the wind continued. The temperature had dropped significantly; cold air wafted down from the window. I heard voices echoing down the hall: Vili and Rodric, laughing and joking. All seemed to be well; at the very least, none of us had been murdered in our sleep.

I got to my feet and stretched, chasing the fog of sleep from my mind. Then I sat down on the bed, used my knife to cut a small laceration in my thumb, and then sent my consciousness to the shadow world.

Once again, I arrived on the plain, in the exact spot where I always did. By this time, the process of getting into Sotetseg was routine: run toward the keep, drops of blood creating a path of "realness" across the dismal plain. Put my hand in the impression to open the door; do the same on the other side to close it. Run up the stairs and command the watchman to open the door. I found myself wondering if the watchman was Lorenz, the sorcerer who had betrayed Bolond. There was no way to know for certain, and the matter was of academic concern. I had more urgent matters to contend with.

I ran across the fog bridge and made my way into the depths of the keep. I'd learned that there were several ways to the chamber where I was to meet Eben; not wishing to meet any of the other inhabitants of the keep, I stopped periodically to listen for footsteps or voices, altering my route to avoid any demons lurking nearby.

I reached the chamber and rang the bell Eben had left for me. This time, he appeared within a few minutes. "Where have you been?" he demanded.

"I came here twice a few days ago, but you did not respond to the bell."

"I was occupied for some time with some tasks for Szarvas Gyerek. More than a year has passed since then. We are running out of time if I am to teach you what you must need to know to defeat Voros Korom."

"More than you know," I said. "I am at Magas Komaron."

Eben's eyes went wide. "Fool!" he spat. "He will arrive in… what? Days?"

"The full moon is tonight," I said. "We have about eight hours until nightfall. A little over a month, as time is reckoned here."

Eben shook his head. "No, it is not enough time. You do not have the strength to remain here for more than a few hours at a time. Have you not noticed how this place saps your energy? It is only by the power in your blood that you can remain here at all. How much blood do you think you can afford to lose before facing Voros Korom?"

He was right: every time I went to Veszedelem, I had to reopen the wound on my hand to produce a slow drip of blood that allowed me to move freely through the shadow world. I was still not fully recovered from my fight with Radovan; if I lost another pint of blood I would be worthless.

"Then we'd better get started," I said. "Teach me what you can in an hour."

"An hour! The fool wishes to learn the secrets of sorcery in an hour! No. It would be futile. You must run. Leave Varastis and his followers to defend Magas Komaron."

"Would it not be preferable to face Voros Korom in a place like Magas Komaron? If we fight him in Nagyvaros, hundreds— perhaps thousands—will die. Even if we can somehow defeat him, our losses will be severe. Do you not wish to save the city?"

"It cannot be helped. Varastis and his followers will not be able to kill Voros Korom at Magas Komaron. Perhaps with your warning they will have a chance of survival, but I doubt it. If we are to have any hope of saving the city, you must return there at once."

"Varastis is a powerful sorcerer," I said. "And many of his followers are formidable as well." I had determined there was little to be gained by telling Eben that Varastis was dead.

"Varastis is a scholar," Eben said with a sneer. "A theoretician. If you wish to hear a lecture on the relation of the passage of time to the flow of tvari toward the void, there is probably no better teacher. But unless he has shifted the direction of his studies over the past few years, he will be no match for Voros Korom. His students even less so. Flee while you can."

"Surely there is no harm in at least telling me how you expect me to defeat Voros Korom? You will have to tell me eventually. Perhaps I can pass some information on to Varastis—unless you are so afraid of a 'theoretician' that you dare not reveal to him your secrets."

Eben snorted. "Varastis has been an annoyance to me, no more. Nothing I tell you will enable him to defeat Voros Korom. But very well. I will give you your first lesson. Do you know anything of the substance called tvari?"

"Varastis told me something about it," I lied.

"All magic relies on the manipulation of tvari. Because tvari is the energy that underlies the existence of all the worlds, it can be used to travel between worlds. Because it is the substance that gives all things their reality, it can be used to alter reality itself, although doing so is beyond the power of all but the greatest sorcerers. Most practitioners of magic employ simpler methods: by exploiting the variation of tvari in different worlds, they open channels through which energy—and sometimes beings—can move. A sorcerer does this by using the tvari in his own body as a sort of lever. Through years of training and meditation, a sorcerer gradually changes the nature of his own body, allowing it to channel more tvari, which gives him a bigger lever with which to manipulate tvari. In a powerful sorcerer, the change may eventually manifest itself in visible alterations of his appearance."

"Ah yes, your gift to me. The markings that disfigure my face."

"Indeed. If you knew what it cost me to acquire, you would not be so flippant about it. It represents hundreds of years of work learning to harness tvari. You skipped over that part entirely. You have the power but no idea how to use it."

"That is no fault of mine. In any case, I fail to see how any of this is going to help me defeat Voros Korom."

"Of course not. That is my point. You understand nothing. You are as likely to kill yourself or one of your friends as you are to do any harm to Voros Korom."

"Very well. Teach me."

"There are many ways to use tvari, many different schools of magic. There are also many different sources of tvari—different realms from which tvari can be drawn. Very few have the power to draw from Veszedelem. In your world these men are called warlocks.

"A warlock can travel to Veszedelem at will. The simplest sort of magic a warlock can perform is to open a temporary gateway between the two worlds, allowing a demon to pass from Veszedelem to his own world. This is a simple matter of making a bargain with the demon. Most demons are desperate, stupid creatures, and they can be bribed with a small amount of a sorcerer's blood, which holds great power in Veszedelem. This sort of arrangement carries risks, however, as you are well aware. If you are not familiar with the ancient accords that bind the demons in Orszag, you may well end up paying more dearly than you imagined." I nodded silently. It was just this sort of bargain that had gotten me into my current predicament. "And if you are fool enough to make a bargain with one of the demons outside the keep, you deserve the consequences you will suffer."

"Is there any demon who can stand against Voros Korom?" I asked. "What about Szarvas Gyerek?"

Eben laughed. "Szarvas Gyerek is far from the most powerful demon in Sotetseg, although his position has improved somewhat since I took charge of his affairs. No, the only demon who might be able to defeat Voros Korom is Arnyek himself, and attempting to summon Arnyek would be like trying to put a leash on a hurricane. Even if there were a demon inside Sotetseg who could stand against Voros Korom, neither of us has anything to offer such a demon that would make it willing to take the risk. No, I'm afraid you will have to face Voros Korom without the help of any other demons."

"How can we possibly defeat him, even at Nagyvaros, if he is as powerful as you say?"

"You must take advantage of his weakness. You cannot harm the wraiths, but their attacks will be uncoordinated. They will swarm around Voros Korom, killing at random. You may be tempted to try to save people from them, but you must not. Their inability to distinguish between civilians and soldiers is one of the few advantages you have. This is why I urge you to face him at Nagyvaros. In any case, avoid the wraiths and focus your attacks on Voros Korom. Voros Korom can shift almost instantaneously between your world and Veszedelem, allowing him to evade arrow and other attacks. You must attack him with something that can follow him through this transition."

"Like what?"

"It is possible to draw an amount of tvari from Veszedelem and imbue it with some of your own will. Do you remember how I blocked the door in the alley when we first met?"

As if I could forget anything from that day. Eben had burst from the rear door of the Lazy Crow, holding a knife to Beata's throat. The gendarmes could not follow because of a spidery creature that held the door shut. I suspected it was the same sort of creatures that had killed Varastis and his followers. "Of course."

"Such creatures are called kovets. They are not truly alive, but simply globs of a shadowy substance drawn from Veszedelem and animated by tvari. A kovet has no will of its own, but a sorcerer can imbue it with some of his own will, in order to accomplish some task. Kovets can take any form, but they most commonly look like snakes or giant spiders. They only have as much energy as the sorcerer invests tvari; usually they dissipate after a few minutes. While they are manifest, though, they are incredibly powerful. Perhaps even powerful enough to bind a demon like Voros Korom, at least for a short time."

"Bind him? What good will that do?"

"It will hinder his movement. He will still be able to shift between worlds, but he will not be able to avoid attacks as easily as while he is in your world. And he must continually return to your world, or the wraiths will die. If your comrades keep up their attacks while you have him immobilized, you may be able to defeat him."

"It doesn't sound like much of a plan."

"It is the best option we have. Hold off the wraiths, pin down Voros Korom, and attack him with all you have."

"These kovets," I said. "They do what the sorcerer wishes, like puppets?"

"No. They are autonomous beings. The sorcerer imbues them with some of his own will and the lets them loose. Once he does that, he has no more power over them than a man does over his grown children. Less, because you can't reason with a kovet. It has no real intelligence or sense. It simply has a goal and some rudimentary inklings about how to achieve that goal. A kovet cannot be recalled and can only be destroyed with great difficulty. Once it has been loosed, it will pursue its goal relentlessly."

"How does it know what its goal is?"

"When you summon it—or, more precisely, call it into being—you must focus your will on it. It requires great mental discipline to summon a kovet. If you allow your mind to wander, the kovet will become confused and conflicted. Its behavior will be unpredictable. Not a few sorcerers have been murdered by their own kovets."

"And how would I learn this discipline?"

"Time. You would start by summoning a very small kovet and assigning it some minor task. Even a kovet the size of a mouse can kill you, so you must be very, very careful. Ordinarily, it takes years to master the skill. If you are particularly strong-willed and single-minded, you might gain a rudimentary command of the ability in a month. In a day? Impossible."

"And there is no other way to defeat Voros Korom?"

"None that I am aware of. There are many other ways to channel tvari, but none of them as effective as a kovet, and many of them are even more dangerous. My suggestion would be that you leave Magas Komaron immediately. Go to Nagyvaros and gather as many allies as you can. Fighting men who are skilled with the bow or spear. Appeal to the Governor himself, if you think you can do so without being thrown into Nincs Varazslat again. By this time the Governor may have heard of the march of Voros Korom across the plain, and he might be willing to assist you. Then you must spend as much time as possible attempting to learn how to summon a kovet. Return here for guidance as you need it. Now I'm afraid I must get back to Szarvas Gyerek before he becomes suspicious."

"That's it? You're not going to explain how to summon a kovet?"

"I just did."

"You said I must channel tvari, using my body as a lever. I don't have the faintest clue what that means."

"Nor will you, until you do it. Good luck."

CHAPTER NINE

I met the others in the room where we had talked the previous night. Domokos offered me some soup and I accepted; it seemed to be the only thing in the castle to eat. The others talked about nothing of consequence while I ate. Domokos told Vili stories of about the history of Nagyvaros while Rodric and Ilona chatted quietly at the far end of the table. When I finished eating, I asked for their attention.

"We have a decision to make," I said. "Tonight, Voros Korom will come with his horde. We came here to warn Varastis and his followers of the threat, and to ask for their help in defeating the demon, but we found only one survivor, who, by his own admission, is not up to the task of facing Voros Korom. I have just spoken to Eben in the hopes of learning something that might give us a chance at victory in this battle, but he was of little help. Eben urged us to flee Magas Komaron and prepare to meet Voros Korom at Nagyvaros, and I am afraid I must agree with him. We don't stand a chance against Voros Korom and his horde if we stay here."

The others were silent. For some time, the only sound was the howl of the wind outside. At last, Rodric spoke.

"We don't disagree, Konrad," Rodric said, "but there is a factor you've not taken into account."

I frowned. Clearly they had already discussed the matter while I'd slept. "What is it?" I asked.

"Come," said Domokos. "I will show you." He got up from the bench and went out of the room. I followed. He opened the door into the courtyard and I immediately saw the problem: the temperature had fallen below freezing during the night. The ground was covered with ice. The sun was nearly halfway to its zenith, low in the southern sky, and seemed to be providing little warmth. The ice was unlikely to thaw today. Gusts of wind reached us even inside the walls of the courtyard; I could only imagine what it was like outside. Trying to descend the stone steps down the mountainside in these conditions would be suicide. We retreated inside.

"It may thaw tomorrow," Rodric said. "We can leave then."

"If we are still alive," Ilona said.

"Is it possible the ice will dissuade Voros Korom?" I asked.

"It is possible," Domokos said with a shrug. "I would not count on it."

"How can we face such creatures?" Ilona asked. I found myself wryly amused at her predicament: an acolyte sworn to eradicate sorcery, she was now forced to ally with sorcerers to survive. Then I reminded myself that I had allied myself with the man who had murdered Beata.

"You cannot," Domokos said. "You must seal yourself deep under the castle. There are hidden passages where the wraiths will not find you. Voros Korom is expecting to find a sorcerer. He has never seen Varastis; perhaps he will be content with me."

"You cannot face Voros Korom alone!" Rodric cried.

"I certainly can," Domokos said. "Perhaps I cannot defeat him, but I can put up a fight. I may even be able to buy you some more time."

"How?" I asked.

"I am no warrior," Domokos said, "but for the past seven years my greatest fear was that Bolond—if that is who it was—would return and do to me what he did to Varastis—or worse. I spent many hours practicing spells to ward off the sort of creatures the murderer used against us."

"Kovets," I said. "But Voros Korom is not a kovet."

"No, but the wraiths are similar to kovets. They are souls manifesting themselves as energy. Wards against kovets may work against them."

"'May'?" said Ilona. "You do not know?"

Domokos shrugged.

"Are you able to summon kovets yourself?" I asked.

"No," Domokos said. "I am no warlock. All I know of such things I have just told you."

"Even if these spells work," I said, "they will not help you against Voros Korom. He will crush you like an ant."

"I also have spells that I planned to use against Bolond himself. They will work on any living creature. Even Voros Korom."

"You intend to battle Voros Korom singlehandedly while holding off dozens of wraiths at the same time?" Rodric asked. "You may as well cower in the cellar with us."

"No," I said. "Voros Korom expects a fight. If we all hide, he will seek us out. If we stand and fight, we may have a chance to repel the attack. If Domokos can hold off the wraiths, I can handle Voros Korom."

"You've both gone mad," Rodric said. "For my part, I do not plan to get near Voros Korom. But my bow is at your service, as always, Konrad. Perhaps I can hurt him with a lucky shot."

"I will fight as well," said Vili. "I am the quickest among us. If I can draw the demon's attention, maybe you two can hit him when he isn't looking."

Ilona sighed. "Then I suppose I will have to fight as well. It seems that sticking together is our best chance."

"This battle is no place for a woman," Rodric said.

Ilona laughed. "All acolytes are trained in combat," she said. "Specifically, we are trained to incapacitate men quickly."

"To prevent sorcerers from using spells," Domokos said.

"That's right," Ilona said. "Such skills may be useful against a demon who can flicker in and out of existence."

"Very good," I said, heartened by the spirit of the group, although I doubted very much that we were a match for Voros Korom and his horde. "Prepare as best you can. Rodric, you will coordinate our defense."

"What will you be doing?"

"I must retreat to my room. I suspect my rapier will pose little danger to Voros Korom. If we are to have a chance, I must try to make use of what Eben has told me."

*****

I spent the next five hours cursing Eben and trying in vain to channel tvari. Part of me suspected Eben had been deliberately vague about the process of summoning a kovet so that I wouldn't try to face Voros Korom at Magas Komaron. Another part told me that my anger against Eben was interfering with my attempts at sorcery.

The truth was that I was afraid to let go of my hatred for Eben, even for a moment. I continually reminded myself that although Voros Korom was the current threat, the demon was not my real enemy. My enemy was Eben, who had stolen six years of my life, disfigured me, and violated Beata's body, ultimately killing her. I had seen him exiled to Veszedelem, but that was not sufficient punishment. Not even close.

But if I did not first defeat Voros Korom, I would never have a chance to get my vengeance on Eben. And if I was going to defeat Voros Korom, I needed Eben's help. More than that, I needed to *trust* him, at least to some degree. Domokos clearly knew a great deal about magic, but he was not a warlock. He knew little of kovets, and in some ways he knew less about Veszedelem than I did. If I was going to summon a kovet, I would have to do it on my own. And I would have to let go of my hatred for Eben, at least for today.

I had been pacing the room anxiously. I stretched, took several deep breaths, and then sat down cross-legged on the floor. I closed my eyes, breathing deep and slow. I allowed myself to forget for a moment about Beata. I let my hatred for Eben slip away. I forgot about Voros Korom, and Radovan, and Bolond. I forgot about my father and General Janos. I forgot about Bertrek, the officer who had caused me to be imprisoned for six years, and about Domokos, Ilona, Rodric, and Vili. I was aware of nothing but my own breathing. Then, slowly, I allowed my mind to drift toward the shadow world.

Before I reached Veszedelem, I pulled back. I had noticed before that it was possible to hover between the two worlds, with some of my awareness in each. It was a bit like balancing on a tightrope: my mind tended to want to go to one place or the other, and the realization that I was leaning toward one tended to result in overcorrection. After several "falls," I began to get a feel for it. Once I could maintain my equilibrium between the two worlds without devoting all of my conscious attention to it, I reached out with my mind to explore that space. If the flow of tvari was to be found, it would be here.

After what seemed like several minutes, I became aware of something, the way you become aware of an after-image from a light after you close your eyes. The sensation I felt is almost impossible to describe; it was as if I existed in the space between the ticks of a clock, a single second expanded to infinity. What had seemed to be merely an insubstantial line, a demarcation between two realms, had become a place that was in some way more real than either of them. And that realness was composed of a vast flow of something that was neither solid nor liquid, neither energy nor matter. It somehow moved without going anywhere, and sustained reality without having any substance. I knew without a doubt that this was tvari.

I reached into the tvari with my mind the way you might dip your fingers into a stream. The stuff that was not stuff was somehow hot and cold, adamantine and insubstantial, moving at impossible speed and completely still. Part of my mind wanted to try to make sense of it. Another part warned me that if I tried, I would go mad.

Some of the stuff flowed into me (or had I flowed into it?), and I felt a surge of great strength and debilitating weakness. I was seized by the urge to get rid of the tvari, or to divest myself of it. But there was no place for it to go, nowhere I could escape from it. It was like being in a cyclone, or having a cyclone inside of me. And it was growing stronger. I managed to tear my mind away from the vast flow of tvari, but the maelstrom continued to howl inside of me. I wanted nothing more than to leave that place, but somehow I knew that if I brought the tvari back to my world, it would destroy me. The "realness" of pure tvari is too great for our world—perhaps too great for any world. It would tear my body apart.

Desperate for a way to separate myself from the tvari, I cast some of my awareness to the shadow world and found what I was looking for. From my vantagepoint between the worlds, I could see the shadowy substance that underlay the world of Veszedelem. *See* is the wrong word; it was as if I was perceiving with some entirely new faculty that had been dormant until now, something akin to seeing or hearing, but at the same time entirely different.

The shadowy substance flowed like murky water into the space left behind by the fleeing tvari. I reached into it, pulling away a glob of the stuff and held it before me. I allowed the tvari to flow into the glob until it pulsed and undulated with something like life. The glob lost its spherical shape, parts of it elongating into stubby pseudopods that slowly grew into tentacles. The tentacles swept about, furiously searching for something to grasp, some way for the creature to apply its will to its surroundings. I drew back in fear, realizing too late that I was falling back into the material world. The thing came with me.

I lay on my back on the floor in my room, with the kovet writhing on top of me. It was nearly as large as I, with a dozen or more tentacles of varying lengths protruding in random places from its misshapen body. It was the color of shadow, visible only as an obscuration of its surroundings. Ice cold to the touch but having no weight, it nevertheless pinned me down by adhering the ends of its tentacles to the stone floor. I screamed orders at the thing, trying to make it bow to my will, but it was no use: the kovet had a mind, or at least a will, of its own. But how was that possible? Had I inadvertently imbued it with intention? As one of its tentacles wrapped around my neck, choking me, I recalled what I had been feeling when I summoned the thing: fear—specifically, fear that the kovet would turn against me. I had made my fear into a reality.

The kovet had wrapped its tentacles around my wrists and ankles, paralyzing me. I could not breathe, and the harder I struggled, the faster my strength left me. My fingers went numb and my vision began to cloud. In a few seconds, I would lose consciousness, and soon after that, I would be dead, killed by my first attempt at sorcery. Voros Korom would kill my friends and destroy Nagyvaros. Eben would never pay for what he had done to Beata. My only consolation was that if I died here, I would not have to spend eternity in the service of Szarvas Gyerek. Or was I wrong about that as well? Would I die only to find myself reborn in the bowels of Sotetseg?

The door to the room flew open and someone came inside. I could not make out who; my head was pinned in place and my vision had gone almost completely dark. As my awareness faded, I heard someone speaking words I could not understand. Then there was a sudden flash of heat and light, and I felt the creature's grip on my throat slacken. I gasped for air. Fuzzy shapes moved around me. I heard shouting and felt fingers grasping at the tentacles around my wrists. Finally the thing came free, and I lay there for some time, coughing and wheezing. I sat up to see Rodric, Vili and Ilona a few feet away, still struggling with the kovet. Domokos stood just inside the doorway, trembling and leaning with his hand against the wall.

I crawled toward the kovet and grasped one of its tentacles, which it was trying to wrap around Rodric's throat. Whatever Domokos had done to the creature had weakened it significantly, but even so it took all my strength to pin down that one appendage. Vili and Ilona were each clutching a tentacle, and Rodric lay on his side, gripping two of them to his chest. The thing's remaining appendages writhed wildly in the air, unable to get a hold on anything. The creature gradually faded, losing strength as it did so, until we all lay there, panting, our hands clutching at vapor.

"The good news," wheezed Domokos after a moment, "is that my defensive spell works."

"What the devil was that thing?" Rodric asked, getting slowly to his feet.

"It's called a kovet," Ilona said coldly. "It's sorcery."

"Sorcery is our only chance against Voros Korom," I snapped hoarsely, rubbing my throat. In truth, I was as angry with myself as I was with her. I could have gotten us all killed.

"This is something you learned from Eben?" Rodric asked, helping me to my feet. He helped me up and the others stood as well.

"Apparently not learned as well as I thought," I said.

"You fool," Ilona said. "You think you can defeat evil with more evil?"

"Kovets are not evil," Domokos said. "But they are powerful. I've never seen one that size. If you could control a kovet like that, it would be a powerful weapon against Voros Korom."

"You cannot be serious," Ilona said. "A monster like that poses more threat to us than to Voros Korom."

"Ilona is right," said Rodric. "I am willing to face Voros Korom and his horde, but I would prefer not to die before they even get here. What were you thinking, Konrad?"

Domokos spoke before I could answer. "I did not mean to suggest that Konrad attempt to summon a kovet to use against Voros Korom tonight. The brand gives him tremendous power, but he has not had time to learn to use it. My suggestion, again, would be to allow me to face Voros Korom alone. Hide below the castle. Keep yourselves alive so that you can face Voros Korom when you are ready."

"That seems wise to me," Ilona said.

"Then you agree with Eben the warlock," I replied.

Ilona shrugged.

Rodric shook his head. "I will not cower in a cellar while Domokos faces Voros Korom alone."

"Nor will I," I said. "This changes nothing. We face Voros Korom together."

CHAPTER TEN

We spent the rest of the day doing what we could to prepare for the attack. Vili, who had spent the most time around the wraiths, had already advised the others how to avoid them. The wraiths had been at their strongest near the center of the ruins of Romok; fifty paces or so outside the ruins they faded to nothingness. If they fed on energy from Voros Korom in the same way, we were safe as long as we stayed outside that radius. Rodric had once been able to reliably hit a bullseye at a hundred yards, but of course archery targets do not move and blink in and out of existence at will. He was the only member of our party with a bow; my rapier and the daggers carried by Ilona and Vili would avail us little.

The wraiths could move faster than any man, but because each of them was composed of the souls of hundreds of individuals, they could be indecisive and slow to react. Vili claimed that by dodging suddenly and doubling back, one could evade them—at least for a time. Having seen Vili employ this tactic with minimal success, I was skeptical, but we would have to exploit every possible advantage if we were going to have a chance at holding off Voros Korom and his horde. Vili claimed the wraiths were also attracted to movement: given two targets, they tended to go for whichever one seemed to have more energy.

The plan Rodric had devised was simple: he would fire arrows at Voros Korom from a distance, hoping to blind him or at least slow him down. Vili would try to draw the wraiths away from Domokos, who would use his magic to repel those who tried to get near Rodric. Meanwhile, Ilona and I would hide in the shadows, looking for openings to attack Voros Korom. Ilona had discovered a staff, which she had cut down to a fighting stick. I observed her practicing with it in the courtyard for a few minutes and must admit to being impressed. I didn't see what good it was going to do against a twenty-foot tall demon with skin like tree bark, though. I supposed she might kneecap him. Of course, I doubted my rapier would serve me any better.

We paused in our preparations for dinner just before dusk. We had seen no sign of Voros Korom, but we had not expected to. The wraiths had no power during the day. In all likelihood, Voros Korom would wait until the full moon was high in the sky to attack.

As the last light faded in the west, the wind continued to howl. The temperature had remained below freezing all day, which meant that the steps to Magas Komaron were still sheathed in ice. As the full moon rose over the distant range, I held out some slight hope that the demon would not be able to reach us under such conditions—and then I saw a glow of bluish-white light undulating at the eastern foot of the mountain.

The patch of light grew steadily larger and brighter, until I could make out the individual wraiths darting like ghostly mantas over the slope of the mountain. From my position at the top of the eastern tower of Magas Komaron, I could not yet make out Voros Korom, but I knew he was at the epicenter of that glow. Rodric and the others stood nearby, watching silently. There was nothing we could do but wait.

The approach of the wraiths indicated that Voros Korom was not coming up the steps, as we'd expected, but rather climbing directly up the eastern side of the mountain. It seemed impossible—there were few handholds and the mountainside was a near-vertical wall of rock in some places—but the wraiths continued to rise. Nearly an hour after we first spotted the wraiths, Vili pointed out a human-like shape clawing its way up the rock. I laughed inwardly at my hope that the walls of the castle would delay the demon for some time: he'd climbed a half-mile of sheer rock wall in less than an hour.

Still, it would take some time for him to reach the castle, during which he would be exposed to attack. Deciding to make the most of the situation, we climbed back down the stairs of the tower and made our way to the top of the eastern wall. The wraiths were now within a hundred yards of the foot of the castle; in the moonlight the dark, flickering figure of Voros Korom was clearly visible against the rock face farther down. Rodric didn't dare risk an arrow from this distance, as he had only eighteen of them left. But Domokos found another use for his magic: speaking an incantation, he touched the base of one of the massive merlons of the battlement in front of us, causing the mortar to crack and fall away. Rodric, Vili and I put our shoulders against the merlon, causing it to roll off its base and tumble down the mountainside. The hunk of rock struck Voros Korom on the shoulder, nearly knocking him off the cliff. But after a moment's pause, Voros Korom continued to climb.

Encouraged, we repeated the maneuver twice more, but the merlons went wide of their target. We were now panting and sweating from exertion despite the cold, and Domokos was trembling from the effort of casting spells. But knowing this was our best hope of stopping Voros Korom, we didn't dare let up.

We had to roll the next merlon several yards to get it into position. By the time we let it go, the wraiths had reached the bottom of the castle wall. This merlon would have struck its target, but Voros Korom vanished for a split second just as it reached him. The merlon plummeted to the ground. We had only enough time to move one more into position before the wraiths reached us.

Domokos staggered to the merlon and placed his hand on it. I was too fatigued to be of any use, so I let Ilona take my place. She, Rodric and Vili maneuvered it into position over Voros Korom and heaved it off the wall. It was a near-perfect shot, striking Voros Korom directly on the top of his skull. The demon's left hand came off the cliff, and for a moment he hung there unmoving, like a stunned animal. So intent were we on the attack that we failed to notice one of the wraiths sliding silently up the wall toward us. Its diaphanous form almost invisible in the moonlight, the wraith had little strength this far from Voros Korom, but I knew from experience that even the touch of a weakened wraith was dangerous.

"Get back!" I cried, and the others complied—except for Vili, who had climbed onto what remained of the battlement. I realized that I'd been mistaken: Vili had seen the wraith. He had been waiting for it.

I sprang onto the battlement, my feet skittering on loose mortar. For a terrifying split-second, I was certain that I was going to slide into Vili and knock him off the wall, but I skidded to a stop a few inches behind him. The wraith had reached Vili's feet, and Vili stood transfixed by the undulating series of hands, mouths, and other body parts spilling out of the apparition. As it rose slowly toward us, I could hear cackles, screams and moans coming toward me as if through a long tunnel. I threw an arm around Vili, trying to pull him back, but dared not move too quickly lest I slip and send us both hurtling over the edge. Vili leaned forward, resisting my efforts.

By all rights, Vili and I should already have been dead. I'd been struck in the shoulder by a wraith at the ruins of Romok, and my entire arm had been paralyzed for several minutes. If the wraith were to move a few inches toward Vili's legs, he would collapse and we'd both plunge to our deaths. But instead, it continued to rise slowly until it the bulk of it was level with Vili's face. The cackles and screams grew louder, and I realized the thing was fighting against itself.

"Vili!" cried a voice from the maelstrom.

"Father?" Vili said.

"Vili…" the voice cried again, nearly drowned out by screams. "Run!"

Vili's body went slack, and we tumbled backwards off the battlement. The fight within the wraith had concluded; it now surged toward us at terrifying speed. Rodric caught me as I fell, and the three of us tumbled to the stone floor. We lay there dazed as the wraith swept forward to consume us.

And then suddenly it was gone.

We got to our feet. Ilona, a few yards away, peered over an intact merlon. "He's fallen," she said.

I stepped forward and looked down. For a moment I thought we were saved, but then I saw him: Voros Korom was lying on a narrow ledge perhaps sixty feet below the place he'd fallen from, his body continuing to flicker in and out of existence.

The demon slowly got to his feet and resumed his climb. He'd been hit on the head with three hundred pounds of rock and taken a fall that should have broken every bone in his body, but he moved like he'd just gotten up from a nap. Dozens of wraiths wheeled about him, darting close to reinvigorate themselves and then soaring upward in an attempt to reach us before fading into nothingness a few yards below the foot of the wall. With each attempt, they got a little closer.

I turned to regard our group. Domokos sat leaning against the battlement, his whole body shaking from the effort of weakening the merlon joints. Vili stared into space, the paleness of his face evident even in the moonlight. The wraith had not touched him, but he, Rodric and Ilona leaned against the remains of a broken merlon, panting from exertion. I had thought I was mostly healed from my battle with Radovan, but I found myself barely able to stand. We were in sad shape, and all we'd done is slowed Voros Korom's advance by a few minutes.

"This isn't working," I said, unnecessarily. "Rodric, ready your bow. Vili and Ilona, retreat to the courtyard. Distract the wraiths and try to buy us some time. When the wraiths get too close, join us in the tower." Shrugging off my exhaustion, I went to Domokos and threw his arm over my shoulder.

As I led Domokos away, Rodric retrieved his bow and nocked an arrow. I heard Ilona behind me, urging Vili to move. I couldn't imagine what was going through the lad's head, and I didn't have time to think about it. Domokos's spells were the only defense we had against the wraiths. To reach the tower in which we would make our stand, Voros Korom and his horde of wraiths would have to cross the open courtyard where we had originally expected the battle to begin. The plan was to get Domokos to the tower, from whence he could see the wraiths advance and be safe from attack, at least for a while.

I helped him across the courtyard and up the spiral steps of the tower. By the time we reached the top, the wraiths were pouring over the battlement we had just left. Vili and Ilona waited in the courtyard, less than fifty yards away. Ilona stood in a defensive position with her stick. Vili, seemingly recovered from his shock, stood at her side. Rodric was nowhere to be seen; I was struck with the sickening thought that he'd been consumed by the wraiths or had fallen off the wall. I forced my thoughts back to my own situation.

"Domokos, are you all right?"

Domokos, leaning against a merlon, nodded. He looked very tired, but he was no longer shaking. He raised his hand as if readying a spell. "I will try... to hold them off."

"No," I said. "Wait until they get closer." I said it almost without thinking, a reflexive tactical response drummed into me from my time in the janissaries. But of course an effective defense would not help us without any way to go on the offensive. If Rodric was out of the fight, it was up to me to face Voros Korom.

The wraiths poured over the wall and into the courtyard. Ilona had retreated into the shadow of the garden at the north end of the yard, leaving Vili alone. Seeing Vili, the first few wraiths flew toward him. A massive hand came over the wall, followed by the head and shoulders of Voros Korom. In another second, the demon had vaulted over the wall, landing on his feet inside the courtyard. His limbs flickered in and out of existence as he had need of them, sometimes seeming to appear in multiple places at once. From my vantagepoint some fifty feet above, I could just make out a small trickle of blood from the wound on his head. It was an absurdly minor injury, but a tiny flame of hope kindled inside of me: Voros Korom could be hurt.

Vili sprinted toward the base of the tower, leading three of the wraiths toward me and Domokos. Domokos raised his hand to begin his incantation, but I put my hand on his shoulder. I counted over a dozen wraiths in the courtyard now, but more were still coming over the wall. Voros Korom had paused, surveying the situation. He had undoubtedly expected more resistance and was trying to discern where all the sorcerers were.

Vili reached the tower, with the wraiths only a few paces behind. He feinted left and then ran right along the base of the tower. The wraiths, reacting sluggishly, hesitated and then continued pursuit. Vili had put some distance between them, but he could not keep running at top speed for long, whereas the wraiths appeared to be tireless. He disappeared from my view among the fruit trees at the south end of the courtyard. The wraiths faded and then dissolved completely as they tried to follow him; they'd ventured too far from Voros Korom.

The vanished wraiths immediately reappeared just in front of the demon; he now had the entire swarm around him. Voros Korom seemed to consider pursuing Vili but thought better of it. He looked toward the top of the tower. Domokos and I couldn't have been more than tiny silhouettes at that distance, but I had the distinct impression he was looking right at me. Voros Korom strode toward the tower.

"Now would be a good time," I said to Domokos.

He nodded and muttered the incantation. For several seconds, nothing happened. Voros Korom continued to advance toward the tower, now flanked by threescore of the wraiths. Vili darted out of the shadows and ran across the courtyard behind the demon, getting within ten paces of him. A few of the wraiths broke off from the main group, but as they began to fade, they seemed to lose interest and returned to the swarm. Voros Korom was halfway to the tower; several of the wraiths, having spotted me and Domokos, screamed upward.

"Close your eyes," Domokos said.

I had just enough time to comply before a sudden flash of light and heat burst over the courtyard, as if a small sun had suddenly come into existence just over Voros Korom's head. Tortured screams echoed across the courtyard. The burst lasted only a second. When I opened my eyes, I saw that Voros Korom had fallen to his knees, his hands shielding his eyes. The wraiths were gone.

Domokos collapsed and I managed to catch him before he hit the ground. After making sure he was still breathing, I lay him gently on the stone floor. It was now up to the rest of us to kill Voros Korom. I looked over the battlement and cursed as I saw that Voros Korom had already regained his feet. The sunlight had vanished. How long until the wraiths returned? Not long enough for me to run back down the stairs to the foot of the tower, I suspected.

Vili had once again disappeared into the shadows. A lone figure was approaching Voros Korom from behind. Ilona. What in Turelem's name did she hope to accomplish with her little stick?

The answer came quickly: she sprinted toward Voros Korom, gripping the stick at one end and drawing it back over her shoulder. She slid on the grass just to Voros Korom's side, swinging the stick as she did so. It caught the demon behind the right knee, causing it to buckle. Voros Korom staggered and fell onto his knee. Ilona, already back on her feet, whirled around and whacked the demon on the thigh. Voros Korom growled, more in annoyance than pain, and swept Ilona off the ground with the back of his hand. She flew thirty feet off the ground, landing in a bank of overgrown juniper bushes. As Voros Korom turned to face the tower again, I heard a voice shouting from the northern end of the courtyard. Vili emerged from the shadows, taunting the demon. As Voros Korom turned toward the disturbance, something flew at him from behind Vili. The demon howled, this time in pain: an arrow protruded from his right eye.

Vili disappeared back into the shadows. Voros Korom pulled the arrow from his eye and hurled it to the ground. He began to walk toward the shadows that concealed Vili.

I leaned over the battlement and shouted, "Voros Korom!"

The demon stopped and turned his head to look at me.

"I'm the one you want!" I shouted. "I am the warlock who rules Magas Komaron!" I wondered if he could see the brand in the moonlight, or if he had any idea who I was. I had seen him up close only once, in the tunnels under the ruins of Romok.

Voros Korom advanced toward the tower again, body parts still flickering in and out of existence. Blood poured down his cheek from his ruined eye. Points of dim blue-white light began to shimmer around him: the wraiths were returning. If I was going to have any chance at stopping Voros Korom, I needed to act now.

I closed my eyes and forced my mind back to the place between Orszag and Veszedelem. Dipping into the stream, I pulled away a supply of tvari. Again I was filled with the terrifying energy and the urge to rid myself of it. But this time I let the fear pass, replacing it with anger. *Kill Voros Korom. Kill Voros Korom. Kill Voros Korom.*

Still holding this thought in my mind, I reached toward Veszedelem for the shadow substance. Drawing away a glob of the stuff, I allowed it to mix with the tvari. *Kill Voros Korom. Kill Voros Korom. Kill Voros Korom.* The kovet began to take shape, tentacles writhing wildly, fueled by my anger.

Then suddenly I was surrounded by hisses and screams. Ghostly faces came at me from out of the void. Somehow the wraiths had followed me into the in-between realm. I lost my concentration and the kovet disintegrated. I had failed.

I opened my eyes to see that Voros Korom was halfway up the tower. Where there were no handholds, he created them by smashing the rocks with his fists. Slowly he climbed, a flickering chaotic mass of hands and feet, blood pouring down his face. Half a dozen arrows protruded from his back, but no blood flowed from these wounds; the heads had barely pierced the skin. The wraiths had not fully regained their strength; still barely visible, they darted about the flickering form of Voros Korom, only a few of them getting within twenty feet of the top of the tower. If I had kept my nerve, I could have killed Voros Korom.

Rodric continued to fire arrows at the demon, but Voros Korom barely seemed to notice. Ilona and Vili stood helplessly below, staring up at the demon. Behind me, I heard Domokos stir. He was conscious and sitting up, but it didn't look like he'd be much help against the wraiths. I was going to have to face Voros Korom alone.

As Voros Korom neared the top of the tower and the wraiths continued to gain strength, I realized that there was only one possible way of stopping the demon. I climbed onto the battlement, drew my rapier and leapt off the tower. I directed the point of the rapier downward as I fell, gripping the hilt with both hands. I'd half expected to fall right through the demon to the ground, dying an ignominious death at the foot of the tower while Voros Korom proceeded to kill Domokos, but both my timing and my aim were good: I landed on Voros Korom's left shoulder, straddling the demon with my legs. The rapier point hit first, breaking my fall, and by some miracle the blade did not break. It sunk into the demon's neck nearly to the hilt. Voros Korom screamed and lost his grip on the tower.

Voros Korom's body tumbled backwards as he fell, and I pulled myself on top of him to avoid taking the brunt of the fall. A massive hand swept toward me as the demon tried to crush me against his chest. Then there was the shock of impact, forcing all the air from my lungs. Everything went black.

CHAPTER ELEVEN

I came to on a gravel-covered plateau surrounded by mountain peaks. Overhead was a dismal gray sky. My chest hurt and the wound on my hand had reopened, but I did not seem to have broken any bones in the fall. I slowly sat up, looking for Voros Korom, but he was gone. Then I realized, as I surveyed my strange surroundings, that I was mistaken. Voros Korom wasn't gone. *I* was gone: I'd been transported to Veszedelem.

It was a part of the shadow world I had not been to before; Sotetseg was nowhere to be seen. I got the impression I was somewhere in the mountains that bordered the plain. Not far off was a rather ordinary-looking stone cottage—ordinary, that is, except for its scale. Although it was difficult to determine exact dimensions without any familiar reference point, I could tell the cottage was unusually large. Was this where Voros Korom lived? I got to my feet and took a step toward it.

Suddenly Voros Korom appeared before me, his face and shoulder bloody. He must have pulled out the rapier, but arrows stuck out all over his body. I started to laugh, but the pain in my chest stopped me short.

"Who are you?" Voros Korom demanded. He did not flicker in and out of existence as he did in Orszag. Somewhere in the back of my mind I understood that this was because time moved much slower here.

"My name is Konrad," I said. "I am sworn to keep you from destroying Nagyvaros."

"You bear the brand of Eben, but you do not have his power."

"Even so, I will stop you."

"You will fail. Even if you knew how to use the power of the brand, you could not kill me. Do you think I can be defeated with a handful of shadow-stuff? You will have to do better than that, Konrad. If you like, I can teach you."

"You are no sorcerer."

Voros Korom laughed. "You may as well protest that a tiger is not a woodsman. I am capable of feats sorcerers cannot even imagine."

"And the price of your tutelage?"

"Let Nagyvaros be destroyed."

"I cannot."

"Why?"

"Several reasons, one of which is that if I fail to protect Nagyvaros, I will be exiled to Veszedelem for eternity." I am not certain why I answered Voros Korom. Perhaps I was afraid he could kill me in Veszedelem as easily as he could in Orszag, and I was stalling for time. Perhaps I really hoped he could somehow spare me from my fate.

"You have entered into a bargain with a demon," he said. It was a statement, not a question. I didn't respond. "There are ways around such agreements."

"Such as?"

"I would have to know more about the bargain and the demon you are beholden to. But first, you must pledge not to interfere with my plan to destroy Nagyvaros."

I gave the matter some thought. "No," I said. "Even if I could be spared my fate, I would make no such pledge. Come what may, I will do whatever I can to stop you."

"Very well," Voros Korom said. "I will return to kill you in a moment." With that, he disappeared.

Our whole conversation must have taken place in a split-second, as time was reckoned in Orszag. Rodric and the others probably hadn't even noticed Voros Korom had been gone. By the same token, though, I probably had some time to get away before Voros Korom returned. He must have been facing imminent danger in Orszag to allow me this respite.

I looked around my dismal surroundings. I'd been to Veszedelem several times, but this time something was different. As I began walking across the plateau away from the cottage, I realized what it was: this was the first time I had physically traveled to the shadow world.

In the past, I had only sent my spirit to Veszedelem, leaving my body behind in Orszag. This time I had taken my body with me—something that only a warlock could do. The difference was subtle. In Orszag, the distinction between spirit and matter was clear, but here in the shadow world, where reality itself was only a ghost of its former self, the soul was nearly as substantial as the body. Had I unconsciously happened on the secret while I was loitering in the in-between? Or had I simply been transported here by my proximity to Voros Korom?

One vital difference between this and my previous visits to Veszedelem was apparent: with my physical body present, I did not need to create a path through the shadow world with my blood. The blood in my veins sufficed. I could only assume, though, that such a quantity of sorcerer's blood would prove an even greater draw to the monsters that lurked in the mountains.

Academic questions aside, the problem was how to get back. In the past, getting back had been easy: I would simply allow my mind to return to my body, which served as an anchor to Orszag. I had lost my anchor. And even if I could send my mind back, I would—at best—manifest in Orszag as a ghost. My body would remain here, where Voros Korom would soon return to tear it to pieces. Somehow I needed to perform whatever sorcery had gotten me here, but in reverse. I didn't have a clue how to do that. I was trapped here while Voros Korom killed my friends.

The one advantage I had was the relatively slow movement of time in Veszedelem. If Rodric and the others could hold out for a minute or two without me, that gave me more than an hour to figure out how to get back to them—and what to do once I got there.

The first step was to get away from Voros Korom's house.

I ran across the plateau and climbed up a low rise, hoping to get a sense of the geography. To my surprise, I found myself overlooking a clump of hills that gradually gave way to a vast plain. Several miles away, visible only as a silhouette against the dull gray sky, was the keep called Sotetseg. If I moved quickly, I might be able to reach it in two hours. If Eben could help me return to Orszag, I might still be able to save my friends.

I made my way over the gloomy landscape, sometimes running, sometimes walking, sometimes climbing, sometimes crawling. The sky of Veszedelem was lit only by a constant twilight, making it difficult to determine how much time had passed. For a while I kept to the bottom of a ravine, as it seemed the most direct path, but fearing that I had gotten disoriented by its twists and turns, forced myself to climb to the top of another ridge. From there I could see that I was headed more-or-less in the right direction; the edge of the plain was now only a few miles away. As I stood there, though, I became aware of something else: I was not alone.

The monsters that inhabited the mountains had evidently not dared get too close to the home of Voros Korom, but now I saw the silhouettes of a dozen or more creatures peering down at me from the top of a nearby ridge. As I watched, they disappeared. I supposed it was too much to hope for that they'd panicked and fled the opposite direction. In all likelihood, they were streaming down the ravine and would soon be climbing up the other side toward me. I ran.

The ridgeline slowly descended and widened into a shallow slope that led to a small canyon, beyond which were several small hills. By the time I reached the bottom of the canyon, I could hear the howls of the monsters behind me. Forcing myself not to look back, I continued running until I reached the hill. Gasping for breath, I risked a glance over my shoulder as I climbed. The demons were still nearly a quarter mile off but gaining on me. I pushed onward.

I surmounted the next hill, and the one after that, finding myself looking out across the unbroken plain. In the distance, Sotetseg beckoned. I ran down the hill toward it. As I neared the plain, though, I realized it was farther away than it looked. Sotetseg was still over a mile away. I doubted I could reach it before the beasts overtook me. I'd begun wishing I had tried to find a cave where I could hide—or at least force the beasts to attack me one at a time, rather than all at once. But I could not hide forever, and in any case it was a vain hope now.

By the time I reached the plain, the demons were less than two hundred yards behind me and still gaining. My lungs burned and my legs ached. The creatures showed no sign of slowing. There was no way I was going to make it to the keep. I turned to face them, my hand going to my side, where I ordinarily kept my rapier. It wasn't there, of course: I'd lost it when I stabbed Voros Korom.

As I waited for the demons to overwhelm me, I was struck by a sense of familiarity. I knew this place. Although the plain was almost completely flat and uniform closer to Sotetseg, there was enough variation in the terrain here that I was certain I had stood in this very spot. The appearance of the nearby hills confirmed it. Every time I appeared in Veszedelem, it was in this same place. And somehow, intending only to take the most direct route through the hills, I had ended up here again. Why?

I had asked Eben why I always arrived in the same place, but he hadn't given me an answer. Was there something special about this spot? Something Eben didn't want to tell me? If this place held some special power, might it be possible for me to transport my physical body back to Orszag from here? My military experience screamed at me to stand and fight, to at least make the demons work for their victory. But I didn't have the luxury of opting for a valiant death when survival was a possibility, no matter how remote. The demons were now only a stone's throw away. I closed my eyes and forced myself to forget them.

I allowed my mind to drift to the in-between place, from where I could observe (if that's the word) both Veszedelem and Orszag. This time, though, my physical body was on the other side of the line. I reached out toward it with my mind, but it was as immovable as stone. There was no way I could pull my body over the barrier between the worlds.

Recalling how I had created the kovet, I turned my mind toward the flow of tvari and pulled some of the stuff toward me. When I had as much as I could hold, I let go, allowing it to flow into my body until it permeated every atom of my being. In all likelihood, the tvari would tear my body apart, but as I was facing imminent death, I had nothing to lose. Perhaps I could at least kill a few of the demons at the same time.

To my surprise, the tvari flowed into my body like water into a glass. When my body had absorbed as much tvari as it could hold, the flow stopped. I still held the other end of the tvari, which now formed a sort of tether between my consciousness and my body. I pulled on the tether and felt a momentary flash of panic as my consciousness moved toward my body, rather than vice versa. I quickly realized, however, that this was only a matter of perception: neither my consciousness nor my body was actually moving; I was closing a sort of metaphysical gap between the two. There was no longer any "in-between"; in fact, there never was. What I had perceived as physical distance between Veszedelem and the in-between was simply the difference between two different modes of perception. I had no more moved from one place to another than a man who first has his hands clamped over his ears and then puts them over his eyes instead. By the same token, neither were Veszedelem and Orszag two different places. They were the same place perceived in two different ways. Tvari now seemed to me not so much a sort of substance or energy, but rather a source of awareness. By tapping into the "flow" of tvari, I was actually expanding my own ability to perceive and act on the universe around me. That universe was made up of Veszedelem, my own world, and an infinity of other "worlds" that were each only facets of reality. And by releasing the tvari, I could allow myself to again to be restricted to a narrower form of awareness, which I would experience as traveling to one particular world. Now that I saw it, I could hardly believe it was so easy. I let my mind drift back to the well-worn track of perception that I'd come to associate with my own world, like a man lapsing into his native tongue the moment he returns to his hometown. The tvari left me, and I felt something cold and hard against my cheek.

Opening my eyes, I found that I was lying on the icy grass of the courtyard in front of Magas Komaron. I sat up and heard a voice call my name. Turning, I saw Vili running toward me. An arrow shot past at a sharp angle overhead. I glanced up and saw the head of Voros Korom, just visible over the battlement at the top of the tower. Wraiths whirled around him, held at bay by flashes of yellow light emanating from somewhere out of sight.

Vili helped me to my feet. Rodric and Ilona approached.

"That's the last of my arrows," Rodric said. "It's up to Domokos now. What happened to you? I thought you'd vanished."

"I'll explain later," I panted, locating my rapier on the ground where Voros Korom must have hurled it. I went to the rapier, picked it up, and ran toward the steps to the tower. So exhausted was I from my flight from the monsters and my manipulation of the tvari that I had to stop halfway up the stairs to rest. Sweat soaked my clothes and my legs were on fire. I heard Rodric shouting from below.

"Konrad, no! You cannot fight the wraiths! Let Domokos—"

The rest of his words were lost to my hearing as I forced myself to continue up the stairs. By the time I reached the top, Voros Korom had Domokos backed against the eastern battlement, wraiths swarming angrily about them. Hovering just above the palm of Domokos's right hand was a flickering yellow glow. It was barely holding the wraiths off, and it faded rapidly as I watched. Voros Korom approached slowly, clearly on guard. Despite the direness of our circumstances, I had to smile: the demon hadn't expected this level of resistance.

"Voros Korom!" I shouted, drawing my rapier. "We have unfinished business!" It was a foolish thing to do, but I couldn't let Domokos face the demon alone. And perhaps if I distracted him for a moment, Domokos might have a chance to fight him off.

Voros Korom turned to look at me, shock registering on his face. He hesitated for a moment and then pointed at me. "Kill him," he said. The wraiths screamed toward me. The light in Domokos's hand winked out. Domokos fell to his knees before Voros Korom.

I stood there like a fool, gripping my rapier, which would do exactly nothing against the wraiths. Having no more tricks up my sleeve, I faced my doom with my eyes wide open. Would the wraiths kill me or merely assimilate me? I wondered if the latter fate would be worse than being a slave to Szarvas Gyerek. I would know soon enough.

CHAPTER TWELVE

A hundred contorted faces howled at me, and I felt the cold embrace of ghostly arms. And then, suddenly: nothing.

The wraiths had disappeared, amid the sound of stone sliding on stone. The howls of Voros Korom receded in the distance. I saw now that a large section of the tower—where Voros Korom and Domokos had been standing—had disappeared.

I ran to the edge and looked down to see the hunk of stone disappear into the shadows of the canyon far below. Rodric, Vili and Ilona soon joined me.

"What happened?" Vili asked.

"Domokos fooled him," I said. "Pulled him in close and then used his sorcery to break off a section of the tower."

"He saved us," Rodric said.

"Is Voros Korom dead?" Ilona asked.

I didn't answer. For some time, we stared into the blackness, unable to discern anything. The wind gradually died and the moon passed behind the peak of a mountain, plunging Magas Komaron into darkness. At last I saw the flickering of ghostly lights far below. The wraiths remained, which could only mean that Voros Korom was still alive. For nearly an hour, the wraiths circled like vultures over a dying animal. Then they began to move slowly north, away from the mountain. We breathed a collective sigh of relief: it seemed that Voros Korom had had enough for tonight.

"Come," I said. "Let's get some sleep."

*****

The next day there was no sign of Voros Korom or Domokos. Perhaps Domokos had managed to save himself, but more likely his body lay broken at the bottom of some crevice. He had saved our lives, but we could not expect any more help from him. Voros Korom lived, and we had to assume that he would attack Nagyvaros on the next full moon.

A freezing wind continued to buffet Magas Komaron for another week. Rodric, Vili and Ilona spent their time telling each other stories and practicing with their weapons. When I felt strong enough, I began to meet again with Eben. He was often unavailable, busy with some task for Szarvas Gyerek or some other project of which he would speak only in the most cryptic way. It was clear that Eben was plotting something, manipulating Szarvas Gyerek in some manner, but I could not determine more than that. In any case, I could only go to our meeting place and wait for him, hoping he would impart some morsel of information about the shadow world or working with tvari. If I was to defeat Voros Korom, I would need as much help as I could get.

The wind finally died on the eighth day after the full moon. The air warmed significantly in the early afternoon and promised to remain above freezing during the night. We spent another night at Magas Komaron rather than brave the ice-covered steps. By the next morning, most of the ice had thawed. We packed up, taking what provisions we could find, and climbed down to the foot of the mountain. Rodric wanted to look for Domokos, but I reluctantly overruled him. We could not afford to waste a day trekking to the north side of the mountain to look for a corpse. If we were to have any chance of rallying a defense against Voros Korom, we needed to get to Nagyvaros as quickly as possible. I swore that if we survived the attack, we would return to bury Domokos and set up a monument to him. Seeing that he would not be getting any support from Ilona or Vili, Rodric acquiesced. We headed west toward the Plain of Savlos.

Ilona said little. Whatever her motivation for seeking Magas Komaron, there was no reason for her to stay. The last pupil of Varastis was dead, and the beacon would shine no more. I supposed this would be welcome news at Delivaros, but Ilona didn't seem particularly happy. Maybe with Varastis dead, she would be unable to use her success to ingratiate herself with the leadership of the acolytes. Or maybe, given the fact that sorcery seemed the only defense against Voros Korom, she was rethinking the acolytes' teachings on such matters. In any case, she seemed resigned to remaining with our party until we reached the plain.

We would not have to traverse the mountains by way of the tunnel filled with poisonous gas; Domokos had told me of a secret pass about ten miles to the north. We camped on a plateau for the night and reached the pass the next morning. It was easy enough to find from this side, following Domokos's instructions. We wended our way along the bottom of a narrow canyon for several miles until we came to a path that zigzagged across the eastern face of the mountain that towered nearly a half-mile over us. At the steeper places, stone stairs had been cut into the mountain. After an exhausting climb of nearly two hours, we found ourselves at the mouth of a narrow tunnel. We followed the tunnel for several hundred yards, eventually emerging onto a small stone platform overlooking the plain. I had been wondering why Bolond had sent us to the deadly tunnel when there was another option, but now I saw: below us was a sheer rock wall nearly fifty feet high, and below that was a steep slope of what appeared to be loose gravel and shale that gradually flattened toward the base of the mountain. Getting down was going to be a challenge; climbing up would have been impossible.

We had just enough rope to tie one end around an outcropping of rock just inside the tunnel and dangle the other end to the beginning of the gravel slope below. Vili went first, climbing hand-over-hand down the rope with his feet against the rock face. When he got to the end of the rope, he let go, landing on the gravel and sliding another thirty feet before coming to a halt, half-standing, half-lying with his belly against the slope. He crept sideways a few feet, sliding nearly as far downward as he did so. I went next.

Heavier and not as graceful as Vili, I did not stop until I'd slid nearly a hundred feet. Rodric came next and fared even worse: unable to keep his feet under him, he tumbled head over heels until he was nearly halfway down the slope. He lay unmoving on the rocks, the blood smeared across his face visible even from my position nearly two hundred yards above him. Vili and I half-climbed, half-skidded down the mountain toward him. Hearing the skittering of rocks above me, I rolled aside just in time to avoid Ilona as she slid past. She stopped about twenty feet farther down.

Rodric was up and moving by the time the three of us reached him. He was banged up and bleeding badly from a cut over his left eye but did not seem to be seriously injured. His bow was intact, but he was able to recover only one arrow from those he had salvaged from Magas Komaron. Rodric wiped the blood from his eyes and continued down the mountainside. The slope was not as steep here, and he managed to keep his feet. I followed at what I hoped was a safe distance, and Vili and Ilona came after.

Eventually we got to a place where the slope was gentle enough that we could walk-climb downward without any great risk of slipping. It was another hour before we reached a place where we could walk normally. Two hours later, we finally reached level ground at the bottom of a shallow canyon. We took a moment to rest and tend to our scrapes and cuts and then followed the canyon south for several miles until we'd reached the place where we'd left the horses. We were relieved to find that although they were hungry and agitated, they seemed unharmed. Ember neighed and pranced excitedly when she saw me, and then reproached me with a brusque nuzzle against the side of my head. We fed and watered the horses from our supplies and spent some time grooming and comforting them. By this time, the sun was hidden behind the mountains and we were exhausted. We made camp for the night. Our location was hidden from view on all sides by hills, so I instructed Vili to try to find some firewood.

Vili returned a few minutes later and told me there was something I needed to see. I asked Rodric and Ilona to remain with the horses while I followed Vili into the hills to the northwest. I asked him where we were going, but he insisted that I needed to see it for myself. As we reached the crest of the hill, I saw why: a few miles to the north, the plain was dotted with thousands of small fires. That could mean only one thing: the Barbaroki were on the move.

"Where do you think they broke through?" Vili asked.

"Kozepes, probably," I said. "The Eastern Army is relying on the Fourth Division to defend the passes at Asztal and Tavaska. The Barbaroki wouldn't have camped this close to Tabor Nev if they were in any danger of attack. Most likely they sent a small force through at Asztal, hoping to draw the janissaries southward, while moving the bulk of their troops through Kozepes. General Janos would not have fallen for such a ruse, but I have no doubt General Bertrek did."

"Then there is nothing to prevent the Barbaroki from riding across the plain to Nagyvaros."

"So it would seem. Come, we need to tell the others."

When we returned to camp, I saw that Rodric had started a fire. Given our proximity to the Barbaroki, I considered telling him to squelch it, but the night promised to be cold, and the Barbaroki would not see the fire unless they sent scouts into the hills, which seemed unlikely. We gathered around the fire and Vili and I told them what we had seen.

"It appears that everyone has decided to attack Nagyvaros at once," Ilona said.

"They will reach Nagyvaros before Voros Korom," Rodric said.

"For all the good it will do them," I said. "Even an army of ten thousand Barbaroki cannot defeat Voros Korom."

"We nearly defeated him," Ilona said.

"No, we did not," I said. "We had a sorcerer and the best archer in Orszag on our side, not to mention a nearly unassailable defensive position, and we still would all have been killed if it weren't for Domokos sacrificing himself. An army alone would be worse than useless against the wraiths. The wraiths will absorb the defenders and grow stronger."

"Looking on the bright side," Rodric added, "Voros Korom will eliminate the Barbarok menace for good."

"Nagyvaros would be better off ruled by the Barbaroki than by Voros Korom," I said.

"What if we warned them?" Vili asked. "They might not be so eager to attack Nagyvaros if they know Voros Korom has designs on it."

"The Barbaroki have been planning this attack for forty years," I said. "They would not turn back now even if certain death awaited them beyond the gates of Nagyvaros. But perhaps we can ally with them against Voros Korom."

"The Barbaroki are our enemies," Rodric said. "I may have deserted the janissaries, but I will not willingly aid those savages."

"It may be the only chance we have," I said. "If, as I suspect, the Fourth Division is more than a hundred miles south of here, there is nothing to prevent the Barbaroki from crossing the Plain of Savlos. Nagyvaros could hold off a small force until the janissaries arrive, but judging by those fires, that Barbarok army numbers at least ten thousand. If they start across the plain tomorrow, they will hold Nagyvaros in a week."

"Then Voros Korom will be their problem," Rodric said.

"And mine," I reminded him. "I am not so easily rid of my burden."

"Aye," said Rodric, his eyes downcast. "I will remain with you, for all the good it will do."

"You've done plenty," I said. "It is because of you that we know Voros Korom's weakness. You've cost him one eye already."

"That was a lucky shot," Rodric said.

"You say that every time," Vili observed.

"Aye, but this time it was true. I avoided the wraiths by diving from the wall into a hedge, and it was a miracle I didn't break my neck. The wraiths, probably assuming I was dead, passed me by. You and Ilona distracted them long enough for me to get to my feet and ready my bow. I had only hoped to hit Voros Korom in the back of the neck, but he happened to look back the moment I fired. If our plan depends on me hitting Voros Korom's other eye, we are in trouble. He won't let me get that close again."

"With five hundred Barbarok archers on our side, you won't have to. I just have to hold off the wraiths long enough for them to get in range."

"Can you do that?" Rodric asked. "Your previous attempt at sorcery was... not encouraging."

"The kovet was Eben's idea," I said. "If we have an army, we can adopt a different strategy. I think I can learn Domokos's trick of channeling tvari into energy that repels the wraiths."

"Learn it how?" Ilona asked. "You speak of conferring again with the warlock?"

"If I must," I said. The truth was that I had only a vague idea how Domokos had held off the wraiths. If I was going to master the spell by the time Voros Korom arrived at Nagyvaros, I would almost certainly need Eben's help.

Rodric sighed. "How many of our enemies must we ally ourselves with before this is finished?"

"I don't like it any more than you do," I said. "But it does us no good to deny the reality of the situation. Even if we can avoid involving Eben, we must come to terms with the Barbaroki. The sooner the better."

"You suggest going to the Barbarok camp?" Rodric asked.

"Why not? I suspect it will be easier to get an audience with the Chief Csongor now than when they hold Nagyvaros." Csongor was the famed chieftain of the Barbaroki. He would undoubtedly want to lead the attack on Nagyvaros, which meant that he was very likely at the camp on the plain.

"Why would they listen to us?" Vili asked. "Even if the Barbaroki know about Voros Korom, they will think it is a trick. They have no reason to believe that Voros Korom plans to attack Nagyvaros."

"There is something we can offer them," I said. "It is unlikely any of the Barbaroki have ever seen Nagyvaros. We know its layout and defenses well. Rodric and I can also give them information on the numbers and locations of Eastern Army troops."

Rodric frowned. "You're talking about treason."

"You need to accept that Nagyvaros is lost, Rodric. We cannot stop both Voros Korom and the Barbaroki. But by playing the Barbaroki against Voros Korom, we may save the city from utter destruction."

"We could ride south and warn Bertrek."

"There is no time, and in any case, our warning would be unheeded and probably superfluous. If Bertrek has not realized by now he's been duped, he will soon. But it will be too late. By the time his men reach Nagyvaros, the Barbaroki will already have conquered it. You and I have long considered the Barbaroki to be our enemies, Rodric, but the situation has changed. The biggest threat to Nagyvaros is Voros Korom, and we cannot choose our allies."

"One might suspect," Ilona said, "that you are willing to side with the Barbaroki because of this foolish bargain you've entered into. You do not care if the Barbaroki lay waste to the city because you will pay no penalty for it."

"Think of me what you will," I said. "I do not claim that the Barbaroki are merciful and just. They will slaughter the defenders and enslave those they leave alive. They will also undoubtedly use the city as an outpost for assaults on Delivaros and the lands farther west. However, they have no use for a city that has been utterly destroyed. We have reason to believe that Voros Korom is untroubled by such constraints. He and his wraiths will kill every living thing in the city."

"Perhaps that would be preferable," Ilona said. "If Nagyvaros is what Voros Korom wants, he may stop there. As you say, the Barbaroki will not."

"Radovan did not summon Voros Korom so that they could rule the ruins of Nagyvaros together. There is something under the city. Something dangerous. That is what Voros Korom is after."

"This is all speculation," Ilona said. "You want to hand Nagyvaros over to the Barbaroki based on a hunch."

"You are free to go your own way," I said. "I will not justify my actions to an acolyte."

Ilona bit her lip, silently fuming. I could see that Rodric wanted to say something, but he remained silent as well.

"I will go," Vili said.

I turned to him, not sure what he meant.

"To the Barbaroki," Vili said. "If someone is to warn them, it should be me. If they kill me, it is no great loss. You and Rodric must stay alive to stop Voros Korom. But you must promise that you will make certain my parents are at peace."

"Csongor will not take the word of a child," Ilona said.

"I am almost sixteen!" Vili snapped.

"I'm afraid she's right, Vili," I said. "While I am loath to admit it, the only one of us they are likely to believe is Ilona. The Barbaroki will take me for a sorcerer, and they will assume Rodric is a janissary spy. The Barbaroki respect the acolytes."

"This is not my war," Ilona said.

"And yet you remain with us," I said. "Why? It is a three-day ride to Delivaros. Go home."

"My... mission is not yet complete."

"You fear returning home because Varastis is dead and Magas Komaron is not what you thought it was. You thought you could ingratiate yourself to your superiors by revealing to them the way to the sorcerers' refuge, but Magas Komaron was a mirage, a beacon signifying nothing. Not only that, but you suspect that your superiors already knew this and have been using the myth of Magas Komaron to manipulate young acolytes such as yourself."

The look of shock that came over Ilona's face was unmistakable. "By the stars," I said. "It never occurred to you, did it? You truly think you are the first acolyte to learn the secret. But then... why do you fear returning to Delivaros? Surely your superiors would at the very least be thankful to know why the beacon has at last gone out?"

Ilona recovered quickly. "No, it is as you say. Of course they knew. I... just need some time to think before I return."

"You have been of some assistance to us in our quest," I said, "and for that reason I tolerate your continued presence in our party. But you are either with us or against us."

Ilona nodded, understanding. "In that case, I will go with Vili. We will warn the Barbaroki of the coming of Voros Korom. I do not think it will do any good, but I will go."

"We will all go," Rodric said. "If we are to have any hope of defeating Voros Korom, we must stick together."

I nodded. "Very well. We will seek out the Barbarok chieftain together."

"That will be unnecessary," said a voice from the darkness.

CHAPTER THIRTEEN

I leapt to my feet and drew my rapier. Ilona grabbed her stick and Vili drew his knife. Rodric readied the single arrow he'd salvaged from our battle at Magas Komaron. As several figures came out of the darkness, it became clear that we were outmatched. One man, his scimitar still hanging at his side, strode toward our camp. He was tall and muscular, with swarthy skin and a prominent brow. By his long, dark hair and the layers of animal hide he wore as armor, it was clear he was Barbarok.

"What is your business here?" the man demanded, stopping before me. He seemed completely unafraid. Glancing around, I counted at least a dozen men. I had no doubt there were at least that many bows trained on us. If I so much as took a step toward the man, I was dead.

"We come to speak with Chief Csongor," I said.

"About what?"

"A threat to his army."

The man studied my face. "You are a sorcerer."

"Who I am is of little importance. My party has just come from the fortress called Magas Komaron. You know of it?"

"Magas Komaron is unreachable. You are a liar."

"I tell you the truth. At Magas Komaron, we battled the demon called Voros Korom. Perhaps your scouts have seen him leading his horde of wraiths across the plain." The man's silence was answer enough. I continued: "Voros Korom intends to destroy Nagyvaros at the next full moon. If you are not prepared for him, he will destroy your army as well."

"It is a trick, Jaromir," said a voice behind the man who had spoken. "They intend to assassinate Csongor. Let us kill them and be done with it."

Jaromir ignored him. "You are a strange party. The woman… she is an acolyte of Turelem?"

"I am," said Ilona.

"And a child and one who has the look of a janissary," Jaromir said. "Are you spies for one of the Eastern Provinces?"

"We work for no one," I said. "We are sworn to protect Nagyvaros from the demon, by any means necessary. The gendarmes do not have the strength to defend the city from Voros Korom. With our help, you may be able to."

"With your help!" Jaromir laughed. "What help can the four of you give?"

"We are familiar with Nagyvaros's defenses and the demon's weaknesses. We can help you take the city and to hold it against Voros Korom."

"They talk nonsense, Jaromir," said the man standing a few feet behind Jaromir's left shoulder. "We must get up early tomorrow to ride. End this foolishness."

"Are you certain you have enough men?" Rodric asked, peering into the darkness. "I count fourteen archers. Given that Barbarok bows are pine twigs strung with mule hair and that Barbarok archers have all the coordination of a palsy-ridden toddler, you may want to get a bit closer. I don't want to be bludgeoned to death over the next three hours by a hundred dull flint arrowheads."

"Watch your tongue, spy, or I'll cut it out," Jaromir snapped. "And then we'll see about that bludgeoning. Your hope of a quick and painless death is fading."

Rodric sighed. "It was always my hope to be killed by an arrow to the heart. I must have angered the gods to face my doom at the hands of men who couldn't hit a sleeping horse at ten yards."

"Rodric," I said, "there is no need to antagonize—"

"Rodric?" asked Jaromir. "You are not by chance the famed archer of the janissaries who once hit three bullseyes in a row, the second arrow splitting the first and the third splitting the second?" I was astounded. It had never occurred to me that Rodric's fame had spread even to our enemies.

"Aye," said Rodric. "I've killed more than a hundred of your comrades. The only consolation I can offer is that most of them died quickly."

"Why do you travel with this sorry lot rather than a regiment of janissaries?"

"It is as Konrad says," Rodric replied. "We are sworn to defend Nagyvaros from Voros Korom."

"You truly consider this demon a greater threat than the Barbarok army?"

Rodric glanced at me and then back at the Barbaroki. "Aye."

"He is not Rodric the Archer," said the man behind Jaromir. "They're bandits. They've concocted this ruse so we won't kill them."

Jaromir seemed uncertain. "We've received reports of the demon crossing the plains, accompanied by a horde of wraiths, but it was heading east."

"Toward Magas Komaron," I said. "It feared the sorcerers would hinder its designs on Nagyvaros. But the sorcerers are all dead. The demon will soon turn west."

"It is a ruse, I tell you," said Dimas. "We've wasted enough time here." All around us, men murmured anxiously to each other.

"That's enough, Dimas," Jaromir said. The man behind him fumed silently.

"There is a simple way to determine if I am who I claim to be," Rodric said. "Allow me to fire a single arrow. If I cannot best the most skilled archer in your group, I'll lay down my bow and you can cut my throat."

I didn't like where this was going, but I bit my tongue. Jaromir's men were looking for an excuse to kill us. If I ordered Rodric to stand down, Jaromir would likely conclude we were lying.

"This is foolishness," said Dimas. "How will you see a target in the dark? And how will we know if you hit it?"

"I will wrap a piece of pitch-soaked cloth from one of our torches around the arrowhead and light it on fire," Rodric said. "Then I will shoot it straight into the air a hundred yards and catch it in my hand before it hits the ground, without ever moving from this spot."

All around us, men burst into laughter. Jaromir's face contorted in anger, thinking Rodric was making fun of him. Surveying the silhouettes around us, I counted heads. There were more Barbaroki than I had thought. Unless—

"Ah, my mistake," Rodric said. "None of you has ever seen a real archer at work. Perhaps a more modest demonstration would suffice to meet your expectations."

"It is a trick," Dimas said. "He intends to signal the janissaries."

"If the janissary army was nearby, you would not have gotten through the pass so easily," Rodric said. "The arrow is more likely to be seen by the Barbaroki camped just over the ridge than by any janissaries, and in any case, help would arrive too late to do us any good."

"You expect us to believe," Jaromir said, "that you can fire an arrow a hundred yards into the air and catch it without moving from where you stand?"

"I don't expect you to believe anything," Rodric said. "That is the point of a demonstration."

Jaromir chuckled. "Fine. Let's be done with this. Prepare your arrow. The rest of your crew must disarm themselves. If you can catch the arrow without taking a step, I will see that you are safely escorted to our chief. If you fail, we will kill you all."

"This is madness!" Ilona cried. "Surely there is a better way to establish that we are who we say."

"I tire of this discussion," Jaromir said. "The challenge has been made and accepted."

Ilona turned to Rodric. "You have done this before?"

Rodric shrugged. "Once, many years ago. Of course, it was during daylight, and the arrow was not on fire."

"But you did it?"

"More or less."

"More or less?"

Rodric held out his arm, pulling back his sleeve to show two small scars, one on either side of his forearm. I had seen them before, of course, but hadn't inquired as to the circumstances in which he'd received them.

Ilona's eyes went wide. "Is that..." She turned to Jaromir. "Would that be sufficient to...?"

Jaromir shook his head slowly, making a grasping motion with his head.

"It's all right," Rodric said. "I'm almost certain I know what I did wrong."

"We've wasted enough time," Jaromir said. "Put your weapons on the ground."

Vili and I complied. Rodric gave Ilona a smile and a nod, and she reluctantly set down her stick. Rodric got a torch from his pack and pulled a length of the pitch-infused cloth from it. He wrapped it around the arrowhead and stuck the head into the fire. When he pulled it away, it was engulfed in flame. Jaromir stood some ten feet in front of him, watching Rodric bemusedly.

"Rodric," I said, "You don't have to do this."

Rodric shrugged. "It's like you said, Captain. Sometimes you can't choose your allies." He nocked the arrow.

I peered into the darkness at the figures surrounding us, trying to think of a way to prevent what was about to happen. I couldn't think of one. Rodric stood with the arrow at the ready. I looked at Vili, who glanced over his shoulder at the Barbarok nearest to him, who held a spear with its butt planted in the ground. I gave him a subtle nod. Ilona stood watching Rodric, apparently oblivious.

"All right," I said. "Do it."

Rodric leaned back, pulling the drawstring tight. He paused a moment to take aim and then loosed the arrow. The eye of every Barbaroki was on the flame as it hurtled into the sky.

Vili fell into a half-crouch and then drove his shoulder into the sternum of the spearman behind him. Rodric swung his bow at Jaromir, catching him on the bridge of the nose and causing him to yelp and stumble backward. I ran between Vili and Rodric, tackling Dimas as he moved toward Vili with his sword in hand. Grunts and shouts sounded from the men farther off. I clubbed Dimas on the temple with the butt of my fist and got to my feet. Ilona, quickly realizing what was happening, lunged for her stick, seizing it and launching herself at another Barbarok who approached with an axe.

Half of the men farther back had already fallen, arrows protruding from their necks or backs. Dark figures swarmed out of the shadows, and the remaining Barbaroki turned to face the attackers.

By this time the spearman had recovered from Vili's attack and thrown Vili to the ground. He now advanced with his spear pointed toward me. I sidestepped, gripped the spear and pulled, causing the man to stumble into the fire. He rolled onto the ground, howling and beating at his armor to dislodge burning coals. Vili dived for his dagger, which lay a few feet from the spearman, but I could see he would not reach it in time. The Barbarok scrambled to his feet, bringing the spear back to thrust it at Vili. To my right, Jaromir advanced toward Rodric, sword in hand, blood pouring from his nose. Farther away, Ilona had her opponent on the defensive; she had disarmed him with a hard strike on his forearm.

Knowing I could not save both Rodric and Vili, I lunged at the spearman, knocking him backwards as he hurled the spear. Vili easily dodged the weak strike and I drove my elbow into the man's nose, breaking it. He fell to his knees and scrambled away. I turned just in time to see Jaromir bring back his sword to strike Rodric. Before he could execute the blow, Rodric reached out, plucked a fiery arrow from the air, and thrust it into Jaromir's throat. Jaromir, his face contorted in utter shock, fell to his knees and collapsed. Rodric relieved him of his sword and beheaded him. Vili drove his knife into the heart of the spearman. Ilona stood a few paces away, the end of her stick against the throat of the man she'd disarmed. All around us lay dead and injured men. A figure approached from the darkness and I moved to grab my rapier.

"Hold, Konrad," said a voice. "You're among friends." The man who had spoken turned to face his comrades. "Casualties?"

"None, sir," replied another figure.

"Good. Finish the Barbaroki. We don't have time to take prisoners."

"Aye, sir." Shadows moved around us, slitting the throats of any Barbaroki who remained alive. Ilona, still holding her stick at the throat of a prone man, started to protest, but was brusquely shoved aside. The man who shoved her ran his sword through the throat of her captive. Ilona looked away.

The man who had known my name neared, and the firelight caught his fierce, angular face, framed by locks of dirty blond hair. I recognized him as one of the men who had been in my squad in the Scouting Corps.

"Byrn?" I asked.

"Aye," Byrn said, grasping my hand. "Then it is you, Konrad. I could not be certain in the dim light, particularly with those strange markings on your face. Were it not for Rodric's telltale braggadocio, I would not have recognized you at all."

I nodded but did not respond. Byrn, obviously unsettled by my appearance, turned to Rodric. "Good to see you, old friend. You've lost none of your skill, nor your flair for the dramatic."

"The wind was with me," Rodric said. "It is good to see you as well."

"Who are your companions?"

I answered, "This is Ilona, an acolyte of Turelem. And this is my, ah, protégé, Vili."

While Byrn greeted them, I considered the his words. I had seen the figures lurking in the shadows behind the Barbaroki and come to the same conclusion as Rodric: only a Janissary Scouting Corps unit would be bold enough to ambush a party of a dozen Barbaroki a few miles from the Barbarok camp. Had Rodric spotted them before I did and identified himself in an attempt to prompt the Scouts to attempt a rescue? If so, he had deliberately forced my hand, sabotaging my efforts to warn the Barbaroki.

Byrn's men, having evidently finished their grim business with the Barbaroki, fanned out to make sure there were no more of the enemy about. I recognized none of them, but by their appearance and demeanor it was obvious they were members of the Scouting Corps. Byrn, who had been in my squad along with Rodric, had evidently been promoted to captain.

I felt a little foolish, having drawn both the Barbaroki and Byrn's men to our location with our fire, but the truth was that if the Barbaroki were patrolling the hills in the vicinity of their camp, they'd have most likely found us anyway.

"I'm surprised to see you this far east, Rodric," Byrn said. "There was a rumor...."

"That I deserted, yes."

"Then it's true?"

"I'm afraid so. If you intend to take me prisoner, I won't put up a fight."

"We've no time for such niceties," Byrn said. "The Barbarok army is encamped just over that ridge, as you probably know. It is urgent that General Bertrek be informed. We followed you because I thought you might know something about the Barbaroki's plans, and because we were heading for the Plain of Savlos anyway."

"How long have you been following us?" I asked.

"A few hours. I was about to reveal myself when one of my men spotted this squad of Barbaroki. We held back until Rodric's diversion."

I wondered how much of our conversation Byrn had overheard. "We are grateful for your assistance," I said, with as much enthusiasm as I could muster. The truth was that Byrn and his men had—wittingly or not—foiled my efforts to parlay with the Barbaroki. If we strolled into their camp just as they were expecting a squad of scouts to return, we would be unlikely to get back out alive.

"Sadly," Rodric said, "we know no more about the Barbaroki's intentions than you do. We came upon them by accident."

"Then you are not here on orders from a janissary officer?"

I needed to be careful. Byrn wasn't stupid, and he was already suspicious of us. There was simply no good reason for civilians to be in this area.

"Rodric and I are working as mercenaries," I said. "We were charged with escorting Ilona to Magas Komaron."

"The mythical sorcerers' refuge? You must be joking." Byrn turned to Ilona. I tried not to let my agitation show as I waited for Ilona to confirm my story.

"Konrad speaks the truth," Ilona said.

"You are saying Magas Komaron is a real fortress? Not just some mountain peak will-o'-the-wisp?"

"The acolytes believe so," Ilona said. "I was sent to deliver a message. Unfortunately, we were unable to find the way."

"No one ever has. In all likelihood because it does not exist."

"So it would seem," Ilona said. "We were desperate."

"Oh?" Byrn said. I raised an eyebrow at her as well, wondering what Ilona was up to.

"The acolytes have become increasingly concerned about the threat of a Barbarok attack," Ilona said. "My superiors hoped to come to a truce with the sorcerers at Magas Komaron so that we could turn our attention to defending ourselves from the Barbaroki."

"The acolytes would ally themselves with practitioners of magic?" Byrn said doubtfully.

"As I say, we are desperate. A great deal of our resources are spent tracking down sorcerers who remain at large in Orszag. Although there is of course no organized guild of sorcerers, my superiors thought that if we could get word to Magas Komaron, we could come to an understanding that would hold until the threat of Barbarok invasion has passed."

Byrn rubbed his chin, clearly dubious. "Then you are headed back to Delivaros?"

"That's right."

"By way of Nagyvaros?"

Ilona looked to me.

"Perhaps," I said. "Why?"

"Be wary of the Torzseki," Byrn said.

"The Torzseki?" I asked. "They don't travel as far north as Nagyvaros." I had some personal experience dealing with the Torzseki; their chief, Nebjosa, had hired me to rid the Maganyos Valley of specters.

"Ordinarily they don't. When my squad spotted the Barbarok army coming through the Kozepes Pass, we traveled to Erod Patak and secured a horse. You remember Artok, who used to be in our squad?"

"Of course."

"I sent him across the plain to warn the Governor at Nagyvaros that the Barbaroki were coming, and that the Fourth

Division would not reach them in time. By now, even that fool Bertrek will probably have figured out that the Barbaroki slipped past him, but it is too late. The Governor will have no choice but to reach out to the Torzseki."

"The Torzseki are savages," Ilona said. "They are little better than the Barbaroki."

"Aye," said Byrn, "but they are allied with us against the Barbaroki."

"That alliance has frayed lately," I said.

Byrn shrugged in resignation. "Be that as it may, they are all that stands between the Barbaroki and Nagyvaros. Assuming that Artok reaches the Governor, and the Governor has the sense to appeal to Chief Nebjosa. You may well encounter Torzseki on your way to Nagyvaros, and they will be suspicious of anyone traveling west."

"Thank you for the warning," I said.

"You're welcome," Byrn said. "I'll also give you another: Rodric, you are fortunate that you are a friend and I am in a hurry. I will not ask your reason for desertion, but it is a serious offense, and I remain loyal to the janissaries. I suggest that once you reach Delivaros, you turn west and do not stop until you hit the sea. Next time we meet, you will not be so fortunate."

"Understood, Byrn," Rodric said. "Must you leave already?"

"Aye. If we stop for the night, we risk missing the Fourth Division as they march past tomorrow—assuming Bertrek isn't still gazing at his navel. I'd suggest you pack up as well. You'll want to put some distance between yourselves and these corpses before somebody comes looking for them."

With that, Byrn turned and rejoined his men. Dark forms moved away from us and then were gone.

"Put out the fire," I said. "Let's move."

CHAPTER FOURTEEN

"That was quite a story you told Byrn," I said to Ilona the next morning, as we rode our horses across the plain toward Nagyvaros. We had made camp about two hours' ride south of where the we'd met Byrn and spent a cold, miserable night without a fire, worried that the Barbaroki would find us. But the night had passed without incident and we were now well away from them. The ground was clear and flat enough that we could travel four abreast. Ilona was to my left, and Rodric was to her left. Vili was to my right.

"He wanted an explanation," Ilona replied. "It seemed like a good idea to portray the acolytes as allies against the Barbaroki."

"Are they not?" Vili asked.

Ilona shrugged. "As far as I know, the Council has no official position on the matter."

"You'll develop a position quickly when the Barbaroki are at your gates," Rodric said.

"I doubt it will come to that," Ilona said.

I wanted to ask her what she meant, but Rodric changed the subject.

"It is good news about the Torzseki," he said. "Perhaps they can hold off the Barbaroki until the Fourth Division arrives."

I nodded but did not reply. The Plain of Savlos was certainly going to get crowded over the next few weeks. If Artok made it to Nagyvaros, the Torzseki would probably be waiting east of the city. In a few days, the Barbaroki would arrive. Maybe a week after that, Bertrek would come with the Fourth Division of the janissary army. Another week would bring the full moon and Voros Korom.

If all these armies could be brought to bear against the demon, they could probably overwhelm him with sheer numbers. There had to be a limit to the number of souls the wraiths could absorb in a given amount of time. If thousands of men rushed Voros Korom at once, a few would get through, and eventually they'd bring the demon down. Unfortunately, there was little chance of that happening.

The most likely scenario, as I saw it, was that the Barbaroki would slaughter the Torzseki and then besiege the city. Nagyvaros was protected on the west side by a bow-shaped section of the river Zold; to the east was a stone wall, some ten feet high and six feet thick. The wall was intended to keep out bandits and raiders; it was never meant to stand against an army of ten thousand Barbaroki. Nagyvaros's primary defense against invasion were the archery platforms affixed to the dozens of spires that towered over the city. The platforms could accommodate nearly two hundred archers, who could rain arrows down upon attackers from a distance of several hundred yards. Against an army of a thousand men, this would be devastating. Against ten thousand, it would be an annoyance. It was always assumed the janissaries would stop any invasion before it got to that point.

The Torzsek warriors and the city's archers could wear the attackers down, but they could not stop them. The Barbaroki would break through the gates with rams and surmount the wall with ladders. They would slaughter the gendarmes, seize the spires and garrisons, and execute the Governor and his staff. They would loot and pillage the city until word arrived that the Fourth Division was marching across the plain. Then another battle would start. The outcome of this battle was less clear to me, but whoever had control over the city at the end of it would command an exhausted and greatly depleted army amid a ruined city with major gaps in its defenses. And then Voros Korom would arrive.

I did not speak these thoughts, allowing my three companions to convince themselves that with the help of the

Torzseki, the city could withstand the Barbarok invasion until the Fourth Division arrived. It was a harmless delusion.

It took us nine days to get across the plain. We did not speak much of our plans while we traveled, but as we neared Nagyvaros, it became clear that we had some decisions to make. We were now only about twenty miles out from the city, and we had not yet run into any Torzseki, which suggested that either the Governor had not yet sent his appeal to Chief Nebjosa or the Chief had spurned him. I announced my intention to turn south toward the main Torzsek encampment.

"Should we not continue to Nagyvaros to warn the Governor?" Rodric asked. "Artok may not have arrived."

"You may do as you wish," I said. "I intend to turn south."

"You mean to go to Chief Nebjosa."

"Yes."

"To warn him of the Barbarok attack?"

"To tell him the truth. If you think it will do any good to warn the Governor, please do."

Rodric scowled. "Konrad, please don't do this. Let us go to the Governor together and warn him of the threat. If he can raise a defense force and rally the Torzseki, the city may be able to hold off the Barbaroki until Bertrek's force arrives."

I shook my head. "I'm sorry, Rodric. My decision is made. Go to the Governor and warn him. But do not mislead him about the dangers they face. If he is wise, he will evacuate the city."

"Evacuate Nagyvaros! Where will the people go?"

"Anywhere else. If all goes well, they can return after Voros Korom is defeated. That goes for you as well. Leave Nagyvaros before the Barbaroki arrive."

"How will we find you?" Vili asked.

"If I survive my battle with Voros Korom, I will not be difficult to find."

"Your battle!" Rodric cried. "Konrad, we are your friends. We will face Voros Korom together!"

"No," I said. "I have been thinking about this since we spoke with Byrn. Without Domokos to aid us, we have no defense against the wraiths. I must focus my attack on Voros Korom and hope I can kill him before the wraiths get to me. You cannot help me, and your presence will be a distraction. Leave the city before the Barbaroki arrive and do not return until you have heard that Voros Korom has been defeated."

"Konrad," Ilona started, "are you certain—"

I ignored her. "Vili," I said, "I promise you that I will see to it that your parents are at peace. Rodric, I thank you for your friendship and your loyalty, but this is where we must part." I nodded curtly to Ilona and she, stunned into silence, nodded back. Knowing that if I hesitated, I might give in to their pleas, I jerked Ember's reins and dug in my heels. She wheeled about and carried me away from my friends. Rodric called after me, but I did not heed him. I rode Ember south toward the Torzsek camp.

Why did I leave Rodric and Vili so abruptly? Yes, it was in part that I feared I would change my mind. But I also did not want to give them the chance to come with me. I didn't want them—Rodric in particular—to have anything to do with what I was going to have to do. As it was, he might never forgive me.

I reached the outskirts of the Torzsek camp just before dusk. There was no sign of any mobilization; the well-worn paths in front of the tents told me the Torzseki hadn't moved in many weeks. Animals grazed loose in the meadows nearby. I was intercepted by a group of Torzsek scouts on horseback, who recognized me from my previous visits to the camp. They brought me directly to Chief Nebjosa's tent without even waiting for me to ask.

Chief Nebjosa lay half-reclined on a rug inside his tent, drinking beer from a large silver mug. He did not seem surprised to see me. He got up, poured me a mug, and gestured for me to sit. I took a seat on the rug and he sat across from me.

"The sorcerer returns," Nebjosa said. "How have you been, Konrad?"

"Well enough," I replied. "It seems that you were expecting me."

"Ominous events portend your arrival."

"Then you have heard about the Barbaroki?"

"Aye, and the demon moving across the plain, accompanied by a retinue of wraiths. These would seem to be the same wraiths that you claimed to have dealt with at Romok."

"The situation was more complicated than it appeared."

Nebjosa laughed. "It always is. Where is the demon now?"

"I faced him a week ago at Magas Komaron. He will soon turn his attention to Nagyvaros."

"On the heels of the Barbaroki, it appears."

"An agent of the Governor has come to you already?"

"Yesterday. The Governor has pledged to give us seven hundred pounds of silver if we join in the defense of the city. I have not yet given my reply. I assume you come to plead on his behalf?"

"No. I come only to give you counsel."

"Counsel about what?"

"The Barbaroki number at least ten thousand fighting men. Even with your help, Nagyvaros cannot hold them off until the janissaries arrive. And if by some miracle you do, your depleted force will then face Voros Korom and his wraiths."

"You wish to convince me *not* to fight for Nagyvaros?"

"As I say, I only offer counsel."

"What is your interest in the matter?"

"I am sworn to defend Nagyvaros from Voros Korom."

Nebjosa chuckled. "But not from the Barbaroki?"

"There is no stopping the Barbaroki. They will plunder the city but leave it standing. Voros Korom will not. The only chance anyone in Nagyvaros has is to let the Barbaroki take the city as quickly as possible. When they do, I will go to them with a plan for defeating Voros Korom."

"You believe you can defeat the demon?"

"I must."

"But you failed to stop him at Magas Komaron."

"I did not have time to prepare. By the time he arrives at Nagyvaros, on the night of the next full moon, I will be ready for him."

"You will forgive me for being skeptical."

"You asked my motivation. I must try to stop Voros Korom. My task will only be made more difficult if the city has already been torn apart by battle. My hope is that if you do not intervene, the Governor will see that he has no choice but to surrender."

"Even if he does, the janissaries may try to take the city back."

"Doubtful, as the Barbaroki would likely be holding the Governor hostage. In any case, General Bertrek commands only four thousand men. He cannot execute an effective assault on the city against ten thousand Barbarok defenders. If he tries, he will still be on the plain when Voros Korom arrives."

"Providing another line of defense against the demon."

"Or a distraction, at the very least. If the janissaries can slow the demon's advance, Barbarok archers may be able to take him down from the spires."

"If they don't stand by and let the wraiths tear through their enemies."

"It isn't a perfect plan," I acknowledged. "But it's the only chance I have of stopping Voros Korom. The less of the demon's work we do for him, the better."

"None of this is any of my concern, of course. My father entered into the alliance with Nagyvaros in a cynical hope of keeping our tribe alive for a few more generations. He never expected the Barbaroki to break through."

"It seemed a safe bet," I said. "Unfortunately, the janissaries are not what they once were. It is my understanding that there was at one time an entire division dedicated to the western part of the Plain of Savlos. Even if the Barbaroki had broken through, they would have faced a formidable battle before ever reaching the city."

Nebjosa nodded. "That division was disbanded when the Governor grew afraid that the people were going to revolt over the taxes levied to pay the troops. My tribe is all that stands between the Barbaroki and Nagyvaros. But we are too few to stop them."

"I understand that you must be very reluctant to renege on your father's pledge, but no good can come from adhering to it. Your tribe will be destroyed, and Nagyvaros will not be saved. I consider the alliance to have been broken when the Governor failed to provide an adequate defense."

Nebjosa shook his head. "The alliance was unconditional. My father, cynic though he was, could be naïve at times. If the alliance is to be broken, I must take responsibility for it."

"Then you will not intervene?"

Nebjosa got to his feet and walked past me to the door of the tent. I followed. Together we stood for some time, watching the sun set behind the hundreds of tents and semi-permanent structures that made up the Torzsek camp. A group of children played nearby, and men and women hurried past carrying baskets of food or jugs of water. Every one of them stopped a moment to bow toward Chief Nebjosa before continuing on their way.

"A Torzsek who will not go to war when duty requires it cannot lead," he said.

"You fear being deposed?"

"I fear nothing. I merely state the truth. I will send word to the Governor tonight, and tomorrow morning I will announce to my people that that the Torzseki will not intervene to stop the Barbarok assault on Nagyvaros. By tomorrow night, I will no longer be chief."

"What will happen to you?"

"I do not know. I will probably be exiled, which is a fate worse than death among the Torzseki."

"I am very sorry, Chief Nebjosa."

"Do not be sorry. It is my decision."

"Do you know who will replace you?"

"I have three sons, but my line is now tainted. The tribal elders will look for another chief among our warriors." Seeing the look on my face, the chief managed a bitter smile. "Worry not, Konrad. It will take some time. The elders will condemn me, but at the same time they will understand the wisdom of my decision. I expect they will select a strong warrior as chief, but only after the Barbarok attack."

"The elders will sacrifice you while benefiting from your decision?"

"Is this not the way among your people?"

"Far too often, I'm afraid."

"Do not worry, Konrad. I do this not because you ask it, but because it is the only way to save my tribe. Your conscience can remain clear—or at least no more sullied than it was before you came to me."

I nodded, returning his grim smile. "Thank you, Chief," I said. But I knew in my heart I had betrayed Byrn and my other comrades in the janissaries. I only hoped it was not in vain.

CHAPTER FIFTEEN

I had hoped to remain at the Torzsek camp until the dust had settled from the Barbarok attack, but I saw now that this would be impossible. My relations with the Torzseki depended on my personal relationship with Chief Nebjosa; if he were deposed—or worse, exiled—I would be in great danger there. The elders would no doubt deduce that I had something to do with Nebjosa's decision not to fight the Barbaroki, and they might decide I needed to be punished as well. The Torzseki's fear of my sorcery might save me, but I could not be certain of it. I had for some time thought that Nebjosa suspected I was not a true sorcerer, but most of the Torzseki believed me to be capable of powerful magic. Whether the elders believed it, I did not know, and I preferred not to find out.

I slept in a tent near Nebjosa's and left at dawn the next day, reluctantly leaving Ember in the Torzseki's care. She would do me no good in the city, and I did not want her to be there when the Barbaroki attacked. There was no place for me to go but Nagyvaros. To the west was the River Zold; to the south was Delivaros, the seat of the Cult of Turelem; and to the east was nothing but vast, empty plain. Besides, at some point I was going to have to return to Nagyvaros to face Voros Korom, and it would presumably be easier to enter the city now than after it was controlled by the Barbaroki. I just needed to find a place in the city to lay low until the battle was over. The Lazy Crow was as good a place as any; its location tucked away in a corner of the Hidden Quarter meant that it would likely be the last place in

Nagyvaros to be subdued. They might not even get to it before
Voros Korom attacked.

I waited nearly two hours to be let in the southern gate. I
could not tell if there was more traffic than usual or if the guards
were just taking their sweet time letting anyone in. I suspect it
was a bit of both. Had word reached the city that the Barbaroki
were coming? Had Rodric managed to warn the Governor? My
inquiries produced no useful information, but that was probably
the result of my appearance and the general unease of the crowd.
Most people averted their eyes when I approached, holding their
children close or busying themselves with securing a load of
produce on their cart for the hundredth time. While I waited, I
scanned the eastern horizon. I suspected the Barbarok force
would not arrive until the next day; although they traveled by
horse, they couldn't move as quickly as my party had, because
they had to pull supply wagons. It was possible that the Barbaroki
would send a group of raiders on ahead, but I doubted they
would. Their best bet was to bring as much of their force to bear
against the city as possible.

As I continued to watch the horizon, moving slowly and
haltingly toward the gate, I began to worry that the sentries would
not let me in at all. In the end, though, my passage was
surprisingly quick. By this time all the city's gendarmes knew of
the man with the strange markings on his face who lived in the
Hidden Quarter. I was tempted to ask the guards about the
commotion but didn't want to press my luck.

When I reached the Lazy Crow, however, I was greeted with
bad news: the gendarmes had arrived during the night and hauled
away Rodric, Vili and Ilona. The innkeeper, Dimka, did not know
where they had been taken. Asking around of the other patrons
and shopkeepers in the area availed nothing. A few people had
seen the gendarmes marching through the street late at night, but
no one knew where they had gone.

I had a feeling I knew why my friends had been arrested: if
they had tried to get to the Governor to warn him of the
Barbarok attack, they may very well have been taken to be spies.
Probably they had been turned away by the sentries at the gate of
the Governor's palace, and then word had gotten to someone

higher up in the government, who had ordered their arrest. It was exactly the sort of bureaucratic stupidity I'd come to expect from the corrupt and calcified government of Nagyvaros.

Famished from my travels, I ate lunch and then retired to my room. Though I dreaded it, I knew I must go to Eben to seek his counsel. It had been over a week since I had last talked to him— the equivalent of two years in Veszedelem.

I sat on the bed and opened a small cut on my finger with my dagger and then forced my mind to the shadow world. I had considered attempting to travel physically to Veszedelem as I had done inadvertently when I was fighting Voros Korom, but I was not certain I could replicate the feat. In any case, I'd found the experience even more draining than when I'd traveled there only in spirit, and if my physical body were present in Veszedelem, I could easily be killed by any of the monsters that lived there. Leaving my body in Orszag afforded me a bit of security: if I faced a threat in Veszedelem, I had only to return my spirit to my body to be safe. On top of all this, Eben would certainly be able to tell the difference, and I was not at all certain it was to my benefit that he was aware of this newfound ability.

As always, I found myself on that same familiar spot on the plain. To my right was the ridge that I had climbed over when fleeing from the place where I'd been brought by Voros Korom. Distant shadows moved toward me. I ran to the guard tower and once again commanded the watchman to open the door. I ran across the fog bridge and made my way into the bowels of the keep.

I found Eben waiting for me.

"You were expecting me?" I asked.

"I saw you arrive. Come." He led me again to the little library, which seemed even dingier and mustier than the last time I had visited.

"What has taken you so long?" Eben demanded. "I had thought you dead."

"I very nearly was. We were unable to stop Voros Korom at Magas Komaron."

"That is unsurprising. I doubted even Varastis himself could defeat Voros Korom."

"Varastis is long dead," I said. I'd come to the conclusion that my only chance to kill Voros Korom was to tell Eben the truth of what had happened at Magas Komaron. I was too ignorant of both sorcery and the politics surrounding it to use any information as leverage against Eben. "He was murdered by a mysterious sorcerer seven years ago, along with all of his students save one: a man named Domokos. He was the only man we found alive at Magas Komaron."

Eben stared at me for a moment. I wondered if he knew the identity of the man who had killed Varastis, but he said nothing more on the matter. "Then it is indeed fortunate you survived. Domokos's magic is weak."

"He learned much in the past several years, but it was not enough to defeat Voros Korom. Domokos was killed, and the demon still lives. He will reach Nagyvaros within a fortnight."

Eben nodded. "Then we are back where we started."

"Not exactly," I said. I proceeded to tell him about the Barbaroki's advance, the Fourth Division being too late to stop them, and my conversation with Chief Nebjosa.

"You play a dangerous game," Eben said.

"I will do whatever is necessary to save Nagyvaros from Voros Korom."

"Even if it means handing the city over to the Barbaroki."

I shrugged, feeling no desire to account for my actions to Eben.

Eben went on, "The question, I suppose, is who will be in control of the city when Voros Korom gets there, and how much cooperation we can expect from them."

"The gendarmes will not stand long against the Barbaroki, if they choose to fight at all. With any luck, Voros Korom will find himself trapped between the Barbaroki at Nagyvaros and the Fourth Division on the plain. If they can be made to understand the seriousness of the threat, they might even cooperate against Voros Korom."

Eben nodded. "A few hundred armed men could defeat Voros Korom," he said. "But only if the wraiths can be neutralized."

"Domokos used a sort of bright light," I said.

"Domokos belonged to a different school of magic, but I may be able to teach you to do something similar."

"Good. But first, I have another problem to solve. Three of my friends are in prison in Nagyvaros. I need to get them out."

"This is a distraction from your mission."

"Yes, and I will remain distracted until they are out."

Eben sighed. "All right. I may be able to teach you a simple spell or two that will help. Do you know where they are being held?"

"No, but I know someone who does."

*****

It was late afternoon when I began my ascent of the stairs to the Governor's palace. The palace was a structure of a type that was unique to Nagyvaros: three of the city's spires, constructed by the ancient Builders, had been united by a vast triangular edifice and a collection of several bridges. It had been built over several centuries in at least five competing styles, none of which was suited to working in irregular triangles. The building was not beautiful by any means, but it was at least impressive as an architectural abomination. I was intercepted at the front gate by two gendarmes with halberds who stared at my face with suspicion.

"What is your business here?" demanded the one on the left. They were both large men; the one who had spoken was broad-chested and nearly as tall as I, with fiery red hair. The other was lean and muscular, with a hooked nose and small, contemptuous mouth.

"I come to see the Governor," I said.

The red-haired man guffawed. "Go home, freak. The Governor has no time for the likes of you."

"That is for the Governor to decide. I have information for him that he will be most interested to hear."

"Give us the message and we'll see that it's passed on," said the tall man, already bored with the exchange.

"The information is very sensitive," I said. Leaning closer, I said, "It concerns a traitor in the Governor's inner circle. I must deliver the message directly to him."

"Oh, then by all means," said the red-haired man. "Please allow me to take you right to the Governor's private chambers. By Turelem's tits, man. Even if you didn't look like a carnival attraction, we wouldn't fall for—"

The man's eyes went wide and he clutched at his throat. His face turned bright red and he fell to his knees. His comrade stared open-mouthed for a moment before drawing his sword.

"Easy, now," I said, holding up my hand. "I've just pulled all the air out of your friend's lungs. He'll be fine in a moment. I will cast the same spell on you if I must, but I'd prefer not to. I am a powerful sorcerer, and I have a very important message for the Governor. I need you to take me to him immediately."

"You idiot," the tall man said, pointing his sword at me. "You think we're going to let you anywhere near the Governor after what you just did?"

The red-haired man was now on his hands and knees, gasping for breath.

"Please, just listen," I said, steadying myself in an effort to keep from revealing just how much the spell had taken out of me. Eben had assured me it was the easiest way to temporarily incapacitate a man, but it had drained a great deal of my strength. If I hadn't needed to impress the sentries with a show of magic, I'd have been better off punching the man in the nose. "The Governor is in great danger. I just need to speak with him for—"

Something hard struck me on the back of my head and everything went black.

CHAPTER SIXTEEN

I was awakened by a splash of cold water on my head. I lay on my side on a stone floor. My feet were bound and my hands were tied behind my back. A sharp point pressed against my neck.

"Pull another trick like that one you did outside and you're dead, understand?" said a voice from above me. I could tell from the echoes that I was in a large stone-walled room, but from my position I could see nothing but the floor and a bit of one wall. I didn't dare move with the sharp point against my neck, but I got the sense there were several people in the room. Despite my seemingly dire circumstances, I felt a surge of hope. Had my plan actually worked?

The voice I heard next was a man's—a well-modulated tenor speaking in refined consonants that seemed to come to me from somewhere far away. It was an aristocratic and authoritative voice. It said, "The gendarmes say you claim to have a message for me."

"Yes, Your Lordship," I said, still not looking up. "It is a matter of great urgency."

"You understand why I would be dubious regarding the motives of a sorcerer."

"Yes, Your Lordship."

"Sorcery is a serious crime, you know. Although it doesn't seem that you are much of a sorcerer, to be apprehended so easily."

"I allowed myself to be apprehended, Your Lordship. It was the only way I could think of to get an audience with you."

The Governor laughed. "You are either a very clever schemer or an excellent liar."

"I am both, Your Lordship. But I come only to tell you the truth."

"What truth is that?"

"Nagyvaros is in great danger."

"You speak of the Barbaroki moving across the plain? I received word this morning. The towers are manned and every able-bodied man is being recruited to defend the walls. Nagyvaros will stand."

"Nagyvaros will fall, probably within a day. Forgive my boldness, Your Lordship, but I suspect we would not be having this conversation if you were confident of victory."

The room was completely silent for a few seconds. Then the Governor spoke again. "Get him on his feet."

Rough hands grabbed my arms and pulled me up. They continued to hold me, for which I was grateful; I was too woozy to stand. The pressure of the sword tip had left my neck, but now one of the guards held a knife blade to my throat. After my demonstration at the gate, they weren't taking any chances.

The room was a vast rectangle, with a ceiling that disappeared into darkness. I stood near the center. The guards oriented me toward one end of the room, where an ornate throne rested on a raised dais. A middle-aged man with curly blond hair and fine features sat on the throne. He wore a deep blue smock embroidered with intricate patterns in gold thread. Next to him stood an older, hunchbacked man with a long white beard, who wore a similar smock, but in gray. In each corner behind the throne was a guard bearing a halberd.

"You are the sorcerer called Eben," the man on the throne said. "I heard that you had returned to my city."

"I am not Eben," I replied, "although I bear his brand."

The Governor nodded. "This was your defense at your trial. A case of mistaken identity."

"You are familiar with my case, Your Lordship?"

"It is my business to be aware of threats to the city's safety. I confess I am in the dark as to why you were released. I've made inquiries but have not as yet received a satisfactory response. I suspect bribery or some other form of corruption."

"I am no threat to Nagyvaros, Your Lordship."

"You are a sorcerer."

I hesitated. For the crime of sorcery, the Governor could have me thrown back into Nincs Varazslat for the rest of my life. At the same time, I knew that my use of magic at the palace gate was the only reason the Governor was humoring me. He was trying to determine if I would be a worthwhile ally against the Barbaroki. He might be willing to overlook the proscription against sorcery while the Barbarok threat loomed. In any case, I had already tipped my hand by using magic against the guard; there was little point in playing innocent now.

"It is true that I am skilled in the use of magic," I said, "but I am no enemy of yours. I am pledged to protect Nagyvaros."

"From the Barbaroki?"

"The city cannot stand against the Barbaroki," I said. "Even with my help. I speak of an even greater threat."

"The demon that walks the plain," the Governor said.

"You know of Voros Korom, Your Lordship?"

"I have received some reports. Before yesterday, the last I heard was that the demon was heading away from the city. But last night a young acolyte traveling with two men came to the palace claiming that the demon would attack Nagyvaros during the next full moon. My guards turned them away."

"They are my companions," I said. "They spoke the truth."

"When I heard about their claims, I sent men to arrest them. They are being interrogated in a room under the palace."

"Why, Your Lordship?"

"I assumed they were agents of the Barbaroki, using the threat of the demon to demoralize us."

"And now?"

"I admit that I am puzzled as to why a sorcerer would risk his freedom for an audience with me."

"It is as I say. The city cannot stand against the Barbaroki. Surrender to them that we may face Voros Korom with our combined strength."

"The Fourth Division—"

"With respect, Your Lordship, the Fourth Division will not arrive in time to save you from the Barbaroki, and the Torzseki will not intervene."

The Governor frowned. "How do you know this about the Torzseki?"

I swallowed hard. In my urgency to convince the Governor of the threat, I had revealed too much. "I have divined it," I said. "The Torzseki will not fulfill their obligation to come to your aid."

The Governor regarded me for some time, rubbing his chin with his fingers. Chief Nebjosa's emissary must have arrived before me with the news of the Torzseki's refusal to come to Nagyvaros's aid. Presumably no one knew about this but those in the palace and the Torzseki themselves. The Governor was trying to determine if I was clairvoyant, a traitor, or just plain lucky.

"What do you know of the Fourth Division?"

"Three days ago, General Bertrek's force was still south of Tabor Nev. It will take them at least a week to cross the plain. Your men cannot hold out that long."

"You know this by divination as well?"

"No. My friends and I conferred with the leader of a squad of scouts near Kozepes."

"This confirms our own adviser's statements regarding the position of the Fourth Division, Your Lordship," the old man next to the Governor said.

"You would have me hand over the city to savages."

"I would have you save your people from a bloody and pointless battle and give the city a chance to survive the coming of Voros Korom."

"You understand that if I were to surrender, I would be signing my own death warrant. The Barbaroki will not suffer me to live, for fear that I would raise an insurrection against their rule."

"I will not let that happen," I heard myself say. It was madness, but what else could I do? I was now committed to my role as a powerful sorcerer. If the Governor would not surrender for fear that he would be murdered by the Barbaroki, I needed to convince him that I could keep him safe.

"You said yourself you could not defeat the Barbaroki."

"I cannot defeat an army, no. But I can prevent them from taking this palace."

"Why would you do so?"

"It is in my interest to save your life. If I am to convince the Barbaroki to stand with us against Voros Korom, I will need your help." That much, at least, was true. I could hardly march up to the Barbarok chieftain after they'd taken the city and plead with him to save it from Voros Korom. The Barbaroki would assume it was a trick. The Governor had some credibility, though, and if we still held the palace, it would give us leverage.

The Governor nodded, considering this. I realized now that he had been resigned to defeat before I'd ever been brought to this chamber. Now, though, I saw something like hope on his face. Whether this was because he thought the city might be saved from utter destruction or because he might still be spared himself I did not know.

"Eben was supposed to be a powerful sorcerer," the Governor said. "But you claim you are not he."

"Eben was once my teacher," I said. "I came to realize that he was a wicked man, and I fought against him. I took this brand, which was the source of his power, and condemned him to live in a world of shadows."

"A curious defense. You say you are not Eben, but then say you are an even more powerful sorcerer."

"I am not concerned with my legal status at present," I said. "When this is all finished, you may have me thrown back into Nincs Varazslat if you wish."

"When this is all finished, it is unlikely I will have such power. Do you truly believe you can hold the palace against the Barbaroki?" he asked.

"Not alone," I said. "We will need as many gendarmes as you can spare. Pull them from the walls if you need to. The walls will not hold, but the palace will. I will also need you to release my friends."

"This is foolishness, Your Lordship," the old man said. "These people are clearly assassins, sent to infiltrate the palace while the Barbaroki try to break down our walls."

"The Barbaroki are not ordinarily so subtle," the Governor said.

"Nor do they need to be," I replied. "Without our help, everyone in this room will be dead by tomorrow. I might add that the Barbaroki are not known for granting their enemies painless deaths."

"I do not think you work for the Barbaroki," the Governor said. "But it is reasonable to think you hold a vendetta against me. You did serve six years in Nincs Varazslat, did you not?"

"The laws against sorcery were in place before you ascended to your current position. I hold the acolytes of Turelem more responsible for my incarceration than Your Lordship, and I am willing to ally with one of them against Voros Korom. You have nothing to lose by trusting me. If I am an ally, I will defend you against the Barbaroki. If I am an assassin, I will at least kill you quickly. But you must decide, Your Lordship. The Barbaroki will not wait much longer."

The Governor regarded me for a moment. "Release him," he said at last.

The two men released my arms and the knife disappeared from my neck. Still woozy, I rubbed the spot below my chin where the knife had chafed the skin.

"Give him his weapon," the Governor said.

"Your Lordship?" asked one of the guards.

"The rapier you took from him. Give it back."

After a moment of speechless hesitation, the guard trotted off. He returned shortly with my rapier. He stopped in front of me and glanced at the Governor. The Governor waved his hand impatiently. The guard handed me the rapier, blade down. I took it, and the guard backed away. I made two dramatic slices in the air.

"Approach," said the Governor.

I walked to the throne, holding the blade before me. The Governor sat watching me for a moment. The blade was inches in front of his face. The guards remained several paces away. I could have slit the Governor's throat and stabbed him twice in the heart just for good measure before they got to me.

"Sheath your blade."

I did so.

The Governor lifted his gaze to the others in the room. "I trust," he said, "that our visitor is not an assassin. Now I suppose we shall find out what sort of sorcerer he is."

CHAPTER SEVENTEEN

The attack came just after dark. The Governor had sent a messenger across the plain to ask for terms of surrender, but the man never returned. I had hoped an organized surrender could be effected, allowing the Governor to pull troops from the wall to protect the palace, but the ensuing chaos made that impossible. Messengers informed us that the Barbaroki had attacked en masse, spreading their numbers along the entirety of the eastern wall. The archers on the spire platforms had expended thousands of arrows, but the sun had gone down and the moon had not yet appeared, giving the attackers the cover of near-total darkness. The Barbaroki had ridden their horses at full speed to within a few feet of the wall, holding their shields over their heads, and then dismounted, crowding up against the wall where the archers on the spire platforms could not see them. While the defenders on the wall threw down rocks and emptied caldrons of boiling water on them, the attackers threw up ladders that had been dragged behind the horses.

The Barbaroki's strategy was by no means perfect: the rising moon showed that hundreds of horses had been slain on the way to the wall, some with riders trapped beneath them. Many other horses bolted, taking ladders with them. Dozens of men lay strewn across the plain, an arrow having found its way past their shields.

But chaos reigned inside the walls as well: the city's gendarmes numbered only about four hundred; the bulk of the defense force were civilians who'd been pressed into service.

Most had no weapons other than bricks, stones and pots of hot water that had to be laboriously carted up ladders. Archers were belatedly called down from the spires, but it was impossible to coordinate them in the darkness and pandemonium. The geography of Nagyvaros is confusing even in full daylight; many of the archers apparently got lost on their way to their assigned posts. Some places on the wall had dozens of archers clustered together; others had none. The Barbaroki took advantage of the gaps and soon had so many ladders in place that the defenders couldn't knock them away fast enough. Within a few hours of the start of the assault, dozens of Barbaroki were on top of the wall. Most were struck down, but enough got through that the defenders were soon forced to fight on two fronts. More and more breakthroughs occurred, and eventually someone managed to get the eastern gate open. Barbaroki poured into the city. The battle was over except for sporadic skirmishes; all that remained was to pillage the city.

I learned of all this second-hand, from messengers who came to update the Governor. Rodric, Vili and Ilona had been released and given their weapons back; we waited together in the throne room, along with the Governor and twenty-six guards bearing halberds. There had been no time for a teary-eyed reunion. My friends were happy to be out of prison, and I was happy to have them on my side again. Despite being given their freedom, none of them spoke of leaving. We would face the Barbaroki together.

The throne room was the safest place in the palace, as getting to it required going through several heavy doors that had been locked and barred. I had no doubt the Barbaroki would get in eventually; our only hope was to convince them it wasn't worth the effort.

The Barbaroki were not an organized force; once they had free rein in the city, they would rape and pillage as they saw fit. A Barbarok warrior hunkered down in a siege of the palace would be missing out on the spoils of war. The chieftain probably had a few dozen men in his personal guard on whom he could rely to help him eradicate any resistance, but even these would tire of a prolonged siege. If we could hold out until morning, we would be in a good position to sue for terms. We would surrender the palace in exchange for the lives of the Governor and his associates. And then, once the chaos had settled down, we could appeal for the Barbaroki's help against Voros Korom. That was the hope, anyway.

As it turned out, I underestimated the Barbaroki's desire to crush any resistance. The Governor had ordered the defenders to pull back to the palace, and the message apparently got through to a few of them. A defensive perimeter some five men deep had soon formed. A mob of Barbaroki, rising to the challenge, threw itself against the wall of men and quickly broke through. The tide of Barbaroki seemed endless; the defenders who tried to push them back were slaughtered, and many simply fled.

We did not need a messenger to inform us when the front gate was torn down. Following the crash were the sounds of a skirmish, which quickly died out. The next door took a bit longer, but it fell as well. Now the Barbaroki were in the hall outside the throne room. The messenger who had been bringing us news of the assault was trapped outside by guards who refused to open the door to him. He died screaming. From the commotion outside, I judged there were at least two hundred Barbaroki inside the palace.

There was not enough room in the hall for a ram, but the Barbaroki eventually managed to hack a hole in the door with axes. Men tried to squeeze through the gap while the guards inside thrust at them with halberds. Other Barbaroki, their frenzy unabated, continued to hack at the door with their axes. The door was now shuddering with each blow; it was clear the whole thing would be in splinters soon.

"Konrad, use your sorcery!" the Governor called, still seated on his throne. The Governor's family and most of his staff had fled to the docks to take a boat south to Karcag Castle, but his hunchbacked adviser, named Bendeguz, crouched fearfully behind it. Vili and I stood on his right and Ilona and Rodric on his left. Vili held his knife, Rodric his bow, and Ilona her fighting stick. In front of us, forming a semicircle two men deep, were a score of halberd-bearing guards. The captain of the palace guard and five more men waited at the door.

I had learned exactly one spell from Eben that might be useful in combat, and it would do virtually no good against a horde of barbarians. Clearly I had to do something, though: our little force would not last long once the Barbaroki began pouring through.

I closed my eyes and forced my mind to the in-between place. I pulled some of the shadow substance toward me and imbued it with tvari, all the while keeping one thought foremost in my mind: *Hold the door. Hold the door. Hold the door.*

I released the kovet and opened my eyes. Men screamed as the dark, spidery thing appeared just in front of our defensive line. But then it slipped away from us and launched itself at the door. It flattened itself against the door, its tentacles spread to the stone wall on either side. The six guards just inside the door recoiled from it. An intrepid Barbarok thrust his head through the gap, coming into contact with the kovet for a moment. His body twitched once and he fell backward, disappearing into the hall. Behind the shadowy form of the kovet, several other men fought not to be shoved through the opening by the men behind them. Meanwhile, axes continued to pound at the door. The Barbarok near the door spoke fearfully to each other while those farther back, unaware of the kovet, shouted and pressed forward.

But although the kovet arrested the Barbaroki's momentum, it would not last long. I wasn't sure I had the strength to summon another, and doing so would only gain us a few more minutes. My promise to the Governor was yet another I was going to break. Not that it particularly mattered at this point: I would die along with him, and whatever was left of Nagyvaros when the Barbaroki were done with it would be destroyed.

The kovet faded and disappeared, and Barbaroki began to surge through the opening. The first dozen or so died almost instantly, impaled by the tips of the defenders' halberds, but the Barbaroki kept coming. The door bowed inward as the invaders pressed against it and finally split wide open. Barbaroki carrying spears or axes now poured in two or three at a time. A few wore helms of steel or boiled leather; the only other armor they wore were leather jerkins or cuirasses. The palace guard were better equipped and no doubt better trained, but the Barbaroki had vastly greater numbers. One guard fell, and then another. Soon all the men at the door had been killed or incapacitated. Barbaroki filled the chamber and advanced toward our perimeter.

Rodric had stocked his quiver with arrows, and from his position on the dais, he could easily fire over the heads of the defenders. He downed Barbaroki as quickly as he could nock an arrow. Vili and Ilona stood in front of the Governor's throne, ready to stop any attacker who got through the line. I had informed the Governor that I was accustomed to fighting with Vili and Ilona, and that having them nearby would help me concentrate on my spells. If he was surprised that a sorcerer would fight alongside an acolyte of Turelem, he did not mention it.

Meanwhile, I stood by helplessly, my rapier still in its sheath. The Governor was red-faced and shouting, but mercifully I could not make out his words over the cacophony in the chamber. I wanted nothing more than to push my way through the palace guards and kill as many of the Barbaroki as I could, but I knew that choice would only doom us all that much faster.

Why had I come here? Why had I believed I could save the city? I was no sorcerer! I couldn't even save myself! It was my fault the Barbaroki had gotten over the wall. Perhaps if I hadn't—

No. The Barbaroki would have broken through no matter what I did. They were not the real threat. My enemy was Voros Korom. I would stay alive to face him. And I would destroy him.

Nearly half of the defenders had fallen, and Barbaroki had started to break through the line. Rodric was dropping them nearly as quickly as they reached the dais, but he was tiring. A Barbarok lunged at Ilona with a spear; she deftly disarmed him with her stick and then broke his jaw. Another swung an axe at Vili; Vili ducked under the swing and stabbed the man in the belly. He staggered back.

I took my hand off the pommel of my rapier and closed my eyes, returning to the in-between place. I thought I had just enough strength to summon another kovet. I forced myself not to think of the Barbaroki coming ever closer and drew away as much of the shadow substance as I could hold. *Protect us. Protect us. Protect us.*

I opened my eyes as the shadow beast burst into being in front of Vili and Ilona. This one was different from the others; more like a floating mass of snakes than a spider. It grew, wrapping around behind us to form a writhing protective wall around the base of the dais. The dozen or so Barbaroki closest to the kovet fell dead instantly as the thing's tentacles brushed against them. The other Barbaroki fell back in terror.

After a moment's hesitation, Rodric continued firing. The kovet's tentacles slipped aside, allowing the arrows to fly through it. A Barbarok fell, an arrow in his eye. Another took one to the throat. The third pierced a man's heart. A Barbarok hurled his spear at Rodric, but the kovet seized the shaft with one of its tentacles and threw it back at him. Another spearman tried to jab at Vili, but found the tip of his spear mired in a sticky mass like thick tar. The few defenders who remained alive rallied and began to push the attackers back. We were still outnumbered five to one, but for a moment we had hope.

The horde parted as a broad-shouldered man in an ornate steel helm and wearing well-crafted armor of interlocking plates of boiled leather strode forward. In his right hand he carried a massive spear and in his left a curved metal shield. Rodric trained an arrow on him, but I held up my hand. I knew from the man's appearance and bearing who he was: Chief Csongor, the ruler of the Barbaroki.

"Sorcerer!" Csongor growled. "Why do you fight for this vermin? This bureaucrat? Do you not know what he has done to your kind? What he will do to you if you survive this battle?"

"Spare me your concern, Csongor," I said with as much vehemence as I could muster. "I fight to save Nagyvaros."

"Nagyvaros has already fallen."

"Your horde of savages is not my concern. There are greater threats than the Barbaroki."

"You speak of the demon that walks the plain."

"Voros Korom, yes. If you know of him, you know it is foolish to continue this fight. We must unite against the demon and his horde before they kill us all."

"Hand over the Governor, and you and the others can go free. Then we will discuss what to do about Voros Korom."

"I will not. Put down your weapons now or face my wrath."

The Barbaroki must have seen my exhaustion, because he laughed. "I think you are not as powerful a sorcerer as you would have me believe," he said. "I had thought you to be the one called Eben, but now I see that you are not."

"My name is Konrad. I am more powerful than Eben."

Csongor laughed. "No, I think not. Look how you quiver and struggle to stand. Stop my heart if you can, Konrad."

"I'll do the honors," Rodric said, aiming his arrow at the chieftain.

"Loose that arrow and you'll all be dead the moment this shadow creature fades," Csongor said. "Your magic is feeble, Konrad. Even now the thing begins to weaken. Moreover, your biases betray you. Do you see how the shadow creature moves to protect your friends? While it lives, no sword or spear can penetrate." He took a step toward Ilona. "But there is one here who is not your friend." The kovet's tentacles writhed in agitation at his approach. Ilona glared at him through the gaps in the barrier.

"As long as I breathe," I said, "you will not touch any one of us."

Csongor nodded and took a step back. "The shadow creature knows whom you love, Konrad. And whom you do not." He brought his spear over his shoulder and, in an instant, hurled it at the kovet. The wall of tentacles parted and the spear flew over Vili's head, embedding itself in the Governor's chest. Rodric let loose his arrow, but not before Csongor raised his shield. The arrow bounced harmlessly off. The Governor, his blue smock rapidly turning dark purple, struggled for a moment to get to his feet, but found himself pinned to the throne. He opened his mouth, let out a gasp, and slumped over dead. The hunchbacked advisor, Bendeguz, threw himself at the Governor's feet, weeping.

The guards who still stood launched themselves at the Barbaroki in fury but were soon cut down. The kovet faded and disappeared. I saw that Bendeguz had cut his own throat; he lay dying on the dais in front of the Governor. Only Rodric, Vili, Ilona and I were left alive. We braced for a fight.

"Put down your weapons," said Csongor. "I came here to kill the Governor, so that there would be no question about who rules Nagyvaros. It is clear that your loyalty is to the city, not to the Governor. Were it not so, your spell would have protected him. Surrender and we will speak of the demon who walks the plain."

I could barely stand, much less fight. Rodric glanced to me, and I nodded. He put down his bow. Vili and Ilona dropped their weapons. Barbarok warriors rushed forward to seize us.

CHAPTER EIGHTEEN

C hief Csongor had us thrown into the same cell where Rodric and the others had been incarcerated only a few hours earlier. Rodric observed that we could have saved a lot of trouble if I'd just requested to join them in the first place rather than trying to get them released. I wearily agreed and then fell asleep.

I awoke feeling parched but considerably less fatigued. Vili handed me a cup of water and informed me we'd been imprisoned for nearly a day and a half. Rodric and Ilona sat together in a corner, talking quietly amongst themselves.

"It's beginning to seem that the chieftain has forgotten about us," Vili said.

"Perhaps," I said, trying to affect an air of hopefulness. "Pillaging a city is undoubtedly time-consuming work. In any case, we may as well take the time to rest and prepare. The full moon is not for another ten days."

We seemed to be the only prisoners in the dungeon below the palace; if the Barbaroki were bothering to take prisoners rather than simply slaughtering anyone who resisted, they were housed elsewhere. We took encouragement from the fact that ample food was delivered by a young slave girl every day. It seemed we had not been entirely forgotten. The slave girl spoke little Orszagish, though, and seemed to know very little about what was going on in the palace or in the city outside. The dungeon was constructed from part of one of the deep tunnels underlying the city; we could hear nothing of what transpired above through the thick rock.

Rodric, Vili and Ilona spent our time telling stories and practicing hand-to-hand combat, our weapons having been taken from us. Rodric was a fair wrestler, but Ilona knew throws and holds I'd never seen before. The acolytes had developed a fighting style that allowed her to use her opponent's strength against him, and although I encouraged Rodric and Vili to learn it, I couldn't see what good it would do against an opponent the size of Voros Korom, and of course it would be completely useless against the wraiths. At least it was something for them to do.

I met again with Eben several times to learn what I could about using tvari. When I was not meeting with Eben, I was practicing spells. I experimented cautiously with summoning kovets, knowing that a lapse in concentration could cause one to go berserk and kill us all. The thought that controlled the kovet had to be both undivided and specific. Conflicting intentions could cause problems, but so could vagueness: when I'd summoned the kovet to "protect us" from the Barbaroki, I'd been focusing on Rodric, Vili and Ilona. I'd *intended* it to protect the Governor as well, but that wasn't what I'd communicated to the kovet, and the Barbarok chieftain had sensed this from the way the kovet acted. I would not make that mistake again.

I was convinced, though, that a kovet—even one as powerful as the one I'd summoned to protect us from the Barbaroki—would not be sufficient to kill Voros Korom. The demon was simply too big and too strong. We needed to attack him with everything we had, and that meant neutralizing the wraiths, at least for a few minutes. Even the full force of the Barbarok horde would be of no use against Voros Korom as long as the wraiths could sweep through our lines, killing or absorbing anyone in their path.

I tried to convert tvari to light and heat as Domokos had, but it was like trying to throw sand against the wind. The tvari simply dissipated, accomplishing nothing. I gathered from Eben's cryptic explanations that Domokos either used a different sort of tvari or pulled it from a different place, causing it to manifest in a different way. I was using the power of a warlock, which meant it was easier for me to work with shadows than light. I would need to find another way to dispel the wraiths, but Eben was little help. He claimed to know several spells that would interfere with the wraiths' ability to manifest themselves physically, but they were all so complex and esoteric that I despaired of ever mastering them. Besides, I was becoming convinced that Eben knew less about the nature of the wraiths than he let on. The spells he suggested seemed designed to work against any sort of spectral manifestation in Orszag, not specifically against the sort of beings that followed Voros Korom. The key, I thought, was the connection between Voros Korom and the wraiths. If I could learn more about the nature of tvari, I might be able to find a way to sever the source of energy that sustained the wraiths. Against Eben's counsel, I gave up trying to learn specific offensive spells and focused on learning how to work with tvari.

When I wasn't meeting with Eben or practicing, I slept. Sorcery is draining work, and traveling to Veszedelem even more so. My frequent trips to the shadow world also warped my conception of time; hours spent there were only minutes in the cell. I would work until exhaustion, sleep until I woke, and then work until I passed out again. I completely lost track of the passage of time. Weeks seem to pass. Then months. How long had I been in the cell? I had just asked Vili, hadn't I? What had he said? Three days? No, that was a fortnight ago. And so it went.

At last a young Barbarok came to our cell and opened the door. "This way," he said, without any ceremony.

I had just woken up. "How long has it been, Vili?"

"We've been in this cell six days, Konrad."

Six days. That meant we had… four days until the full moon?

"Hurry up," the Barbarok said. "The chieftain won't wait all day."

So at last we were going to be taken to the chieftain to determine our strategy for dealing with Voros Korom. It was none too soon. We filed out of the cell. The Barbarok gestured for us to go back up the passage through which we had entered. We did so.

We were taken to Chief Csongor, who sat with several other Barbaroki in a high-ceilinged room dominated by a large wooden table. Spread across the table were several maps painted on vellum; a young Barbarok man began rolling them up as we were escorted inside.

"Ah, the great sorcerer, Konrad, has arrived," Csongor said. "Please, sit. What is your plan to save the city, sorcerer?"

I pulled out a chair and sat. Rodric took a seat to my left, and Vili and Ilona to my left.

"I have been practicing my craft," I said. "I believe I can find a weakness in the wraiths. They are dependent for their existence on a flow of energy from Voros Korom. If I can sever that flow, I can destroy them. Once the wraiths are eliminated, defeating Voros Korom will be no great challenge, if we have enough men. I assume by now you have subjugated the entire city?"

"Pockets of resistance remain, but they are of no great concern. We have not penetrated the Hidden Quarter, but I understand there is little wealth there."

While I was glad to hear the Hidden Quarter had been spared the ravages of the Barbaroki, I was puzzled by Csongor's statement. "Will you not have to take the Hidden Quarter eventually in order to hold the city?"

"If I intended to hold the city, yes."

I felt a tightness in my chest. All along, I had assumed the Barbaroki intended to seize Nagyvaros to establish a foothold to take the other cities along the Zold. It never occurred to me that they might plunder the city and leave.

"When will you go?"

"Preparations are being made now. We have taken what we can from the city and will head south tomorrow."

"You fear the janissaries."

"I fear nothing, but I suppose it unwise to expend so much effort to defend a city that is doomed to be destroyed by a demon."

"What do you know of Voros Korom?"

"Enough. Did you think it a coincidence that we attacked only a few days before his coming? The plan had long been in place, but we had considered it too risky to implement. We were not certain the janissaries would fall for the ruse, but one of your kind warned us that if we intended to break through the janissary line, we would need to do it quickly."

"One of my kind?" I asked. "A sorcerer?"

"So it appeared. He employed a spell to keep his face in shadow. We did not trust him, but he demonstrated his power to us. He caused an army of phantom warriors to appear before us, so real that my men charged them and many fell over each other trying to kill the phantoms. He used this same trick to fool General Bertrek into sending his men southward."

The strange convergence of foes on Nagyvaros began to make more sense. But who could the mysterious sorcerer be? Had Radovan lived? Or was it once again the insane Bolond working his mischief?

"If you can hold Nagyvaros," I said, "you will be unstoppable. The Barbaroki could take every city along the Zold and continue west."

"It is not worth the risk. When I saw that the Governor had a sorcerer in his employ, I considered making a stand here, but I am not certain you have the power to vanquish the wraiths. The Barbaroki are fierce warriors, but they are not prepared to fight demons and ghosts. We will make Delivaros our home."

"No!" cried Ilona. "Delivaros is no threat to you. We have remained neutral in the affairs of the Eastern Kingdoms for centuries and have always treated the Barbaroki with respect."

"The acolytes are neutral when it suits them," said Csongor. "Your persecution of sorcerers is selective, favoring kingdoms that are deferential to you. Even now, you consort with a sorcerer, although to what end I do not know."

"I am not here as a representative of the acolytes."

"Then do not speak as if you are," Csongor snapped. "Enough of this. Delivaros will be mine. I have summoned you here one reason. Indeed, there is but one reason you still live: I do not trust sorcerers, but I am even more loath to deal with demons. If by some miracle you are able to hold the city against Voros Korom, I want you to remember that I let you live."

"You want us to be grateful to you for leaving us to die at the hands of Voros Korom?" Rodric asked.

Csongor shrugged. "If you die, your gratitude is of no concern. If you live, then it is in part because I did not kill you along with the Governor and his men. I only suggest that we might form an alliance in the future. If you successfully deal with the demon, you will have removed a threat to my rule in Orszag. Gratitude runs both ways. Now I must ask you to excuse me. There are many things I must address if we are to leave the city tomorrow."

By this time the assistant had finished rolling up the maps and left the room. Now Csongor walked out as well, leaving the four of us alone. For some time, we sat in silence.

"What do we do now?" Vili asked at last. The palace was strangely quiet, as if it were nearly deserted.

"We cannot face Voros Korom alone," Rodric said. "It is madness." Ilona, still in shock about the possibility of the Barbaroki attacking Delivaros, said nothing.

"With some luck," I said, "we will not have to. Did you see those maps? On one of them, the location of the Fourth Division had been marked with a grease pencil. If that map was accurate, General Bertrek's force will be here by tomorrow. That is why the Barbaroki are in such a hurry to leave."

"But Bertrek will want to pursue the Barbaroki south," Rodric said. "He will not station his men in a city that has already fallen."

"We only need him to leave a small contingent of archers. Enough to overwhelm Voros Korom when I neutralize the wraiths."

"*If* you neutralize them," Rodric said. "How many archers do you think we will need?"

"I'd like five hundred," I said. "But a hundred might suffice. The way Voros Korom blinks in and out of existence, he's difficult to hit, and his skin is so thick that most of the arrows will hurt him no more than a splinter. But we've proven that he *can* be hurt. We just need to keep up the pressure."

"There remains one other problem," Rodric said. "Who is going to convince General Bertrek to leave five hundred of his men behind? I'm a deserter, and he's certainly not going to trust the man he had sent to prison for six years on false charges. Vili's just a child." Vili looked like he wanted to protest but bit his tongue. We all looked to Ilona.

"You cannot be serious," Ilona said. "The Barbaroki are about to attack my home, and you want me to beg the only man who can save it to leave some of his troops behind to fight a demon? This city is lost. If you still wish to do some good, let us go to Delivaros and make our stand there."

"My fate is here," I said.

"That is because you are a sorcerer. You deny it when it suits you, but you are already well down that path. And we have all seen where it leads. If you try to face this demon with more magic, you will only make things worse."

"It is only because of magic that you are alive," I reminded her. "Domokos saved all of our lives at Magas Komaron."

"Then perhaps it would be better if I were dead. I have done no one any good since I left Delivaros."

"Why did you leave?" Rodric asked. "Why did you seek Magas Komaron? It is clear you were not acting on orders from the Council."

Ilona shook her head. "It doesn't matter. I was wrong to leave. I must return home and face the consequences. Maybe I can still do something to help save Delivaros."

"I do not believe it was a mistake," Rodric said. "Without you, we would never have made it to Magas Komaron. We would never have learned all we now know about Voros Korom. There has to be a reason for that. Maybe, if we work together, we can still defeat him."

"You speak of fate," Ilona said.

"I am no philosopher," Rodric said, "but my understanding is that the acolytes of Turelem oppose sorcery because they believe there are powers with which mortals should not meddle. But if that is the case, does it not imply that there is some authority above us who reserves that power for themselves? And if so, then—assuming that power is to be considered worthy of respect—does it not mean that someone is watching out for us?"

I couldn't help laughing. "You wax quite metaphysical for a non-philosopher, Rodric."

Rodric blushed, but Ilona nodded. "No, he is right. The words are crude, but he expresses the essence of the acolytes' opposition to sorcery. We believe that only those such as the Blessed Mother, who have ascended to a state of moral perfection, have the right to employ the mysterious energy that underlies our universe. We trust her to guide us and use events to work together for the good of the faithful."

"Then is it not possible," I said, "that Turelem herself arranged for you to ally with a sorcerer?"

"That is blasphemy," Ilona said curtly.

"Be that as it may," I said, "sorcery is our only hope against Voros Korom. Sorcery and several hundred archers, Turelem willing. I will not pretend to understand your faith, but neither do you understand what I have been through. I ask only this: make a decision, one way or another. Stay with us and fight Voros Korom however we can, or return to Delivaros."

Ilona nodded sadly. "In this we can agree: my dithering serves neither of us. I will return to Delivaros in the morning."

CHAPTER NINETEEN

We spent the night in an unused suite in the palace. It was mostly empty by this point, but enough Barbaroki remained that we didn't fear anyone coming in to ransack the place. Csongor had made it clear that we were not to be harmed.

The rest of Csongor's men were gone by late morning, and by noon the city was rid of the Barbaroki—as well as much of its wealth. The invaders had plundered the palace and other government buildings, the temples, the homes of the wealthier residents (and many of the less wealthy), and most of the markets and storehouses. What the Barbaroki left behind was stolen by opportunistic looters. The few gendarmes who hadn't been killed had gone into hiding.

Rodric, Vili and I could not hold the palace alone, so we stocked up on supplies from what little the Barbaroki had left in the palace's stores and set out across the city. By this time the worst of the looting was over. Corpses of humans and horses, swarming with flies, lay strewn in the streets, and weeping could be heard in the distance. A man wandered by in a daze, his face crusted with dried blood, calling the name of his wife. The air was thick with the smoke from a dozen fires across the city. Only Nagyvaros's unique construction saved it from being entirely consumed: most of the larger buildings were composed of the stone-like aggregate used by the Builders, and the many chasms and walls throughout the city served as firebreaks. Still, I could not help but think of my dream about the city being consumed by flame. If the dream had been a portent, it was mistaken: Nagyvaros could not burn. But what had happened to it was arguably worse. People had been slaughtered, families torn apart, women and children enslaved by the Barbaroki. And as in the dream, I had stood by and allowed it to happen.

As we made our way through the refuse-cluttered streets, an old woman, dressed only in a ragged wool blanket, approached and stopped before us. "Sorcerer!" she cried, her voice hoarse and shrill. "Why didn't you stop this?"

I didn't recognize the woman, but by this time many in the city knew of the man with strange markings on his face, who many claimed was a sorcerer. Having no answer, I averted my eyes and walked past. Rodric, on my right, slipped past the woman, giving her a polite nod.

"No answer, sorcerer?" shouted a man's voice from my left. I looked past Vili to see a middle-aged man collecting bruised apples in a burlap sack from where they'd spilled onto the street. "You and your friends look quite well. Been getting plenty of rest lately, have you?"

Several other people on the street had stopped to stare at us. I kept moving, realizing that things could get ugly if enough people tried to block our way.

"That's right," shouted the man. "Run away. This is why nobody trusts you lot. They should have let you rot in that salt mine!"

We pushed through the crowd and were once again on an open part of the street. I'd been tempted to answer, but what could I say? They were right; we'd done nothing to save the city. Worse than that, I'd had a hand in the city's destruction. If I hadn't intervened—or had begged Nebjosa to make a stand against the Barbaroki—Nagyvaros might have been saved. The Torzseki would have been crushed, but the Barbaroki's advance might have been delayed enough that they would still be in the city when the Fourth Division arrived. The Barbaroki could easily have held the city against the janissaries for a week. When Voros Korom arrived, he would have to break through the Fourth Division on the plain and then defeat the Barbaroki in the city. Of course, General Bertrek would probably have ordered his men to stand down and allow Voros Korom into the city, hoping the demon would take care of the Barbaroki for him....

I forced the thought from my mind. Such speculation was useless. The fact was, I'd miscalculated, counting on the Barbaroki's desire to hold Nagyvaros for strategic purposes. What I hadn't known—but should have realized—was that the coming of the Barbaroki a few days in advance of Voros Korom was not a coincidence. Csongor had known about Voros Korom, because someone had warned him. If that someone was Bolond, what was his angle? Was he simply wreaking mischief at random, or had he manipulated the Barbaroki into laying waste to Nagyvaros to clear the way for Voros Korom?

That had certainly been the result. The city was defenseless and in shambles. No mere wall would keep out Voros Korom and his wraiths in any case, but the city guard might have at least slowed him down. As things stood, Voros Korom could walk right in and take up residence in the palace if he so desired.

We continued to the eastern gate, which stood open, hanging from broken hinges. There were few people around; evidently most of those who intended to flee the chaos had already done so. Once outside the city, we said a curt goodbye to Ilona. Again, what was there to say? It seemed that our paths had crossed not because of the machinations of fate or providence, but rather as a result of blind chance. We had found the way to Magas Komaron, but it had availed us nothing. We could not save Nagyvaros, and soon Delivaros would fall to the Barbaroki. I could see that Rodric wanted to say something more to Ilona, perhaps offer to go with her to Delivaros, but he did not. He watched silently as she turned and walked away down the road to the south. None of us had horses; Ember remained with the Torzseki, and the other horses had been taken from their stable by the Barbaroki. It would take Ilona three days to get to Delivaros on foot, by which time it would most likely already have fallen to the Barbaroki. Delivaros had minimal defenses; it relied for protection on its relationship with Nagyvaros and its position as the seat of the politically powerful Cult of Turelem. The Barbaroki, however, did not care about such political concerns.

Rodric, Vili and I traveled east across the plain until we found a place along the Sebastis creek where we could camp. We spent a night there and then I set out again. Rodric and Vili would wait there while I sought out the janissaries. I took off my cloak and put on an old tattered ceremonial robe that the Barbaroki had left behind in the palace. I felt like a fool, but without Ilona to make the appeal to General Bertrek, our best bet was for me to fully embrace the role of sorcerer. It had been six years since I had seen Bertrek; with any luck, he wouldn't recognize me. Whether he would accede to my request—or even deign to meet with me—was another question. I reluctantly left my rapier and scabbard with Rodric, pulled the robe's hood over my head, and started out across the plain.

I had only a rough idea where the Fourth Division was; I was estimating based on my knowledge of their last known position and the fastest route over the plain. It was entirely possible I would pass right by them a few miles to the north or south. When I hadn't encountered them by late afternoon, I began to wonder if I should change course. But then I saw four men on horseback coming toward me over the plain. It soon became clear that they were a forward scouting party for the janissaries. They encircled me and demanded to know who I was and what I was doing. I told them I was the sorcerer Samvel and that I had a message for General Bertrek. Amused, they escorted me three miles to the janissary camp.

I was forced to wait under guard just outside the camp for nearly two hours. When the general's adjutant finally came for me, it was cold and dark, and the camp was illuminated by torches and cooking fires. I was checked for weapons and escorted past several hundred tents to General Bertrek's tent. In daylight I might have recognized some of the men, but at night they were interchangeable shadows. They joked and spoke in the overly jovial way soldiers did when they were nervous about an upcoming battle. None of them paid me any mind.

Clearly neither Bertrek nor his aides considered me a threat. I wondered if they had heard any stories about the crazy sorcerer who wandered the streets of Nagyvaros. I thought it unlikely. Probably they considered me a curiosity or a source of entertainment. Fortunately, they did not seem to have concluded I was a Barbarok spy.

Bertrek was seated at his desk when I was escorted into his tent. It was the same desk that had once belonged to my old friend and mentor, General Janos. I felt a momentary pang of nostalgia. How much simpler the world had seemed back then, when all my energies were devoted to finding my way back to Beata. I put such thoughts out of my mind.

"General Bertrek," I said, resisting the urge to salute. I held Bertrek in low esteem, but the reflex to salute a superior officer was deeply ingrained. I was here not as a soldier, but as a sorcerer.

"By Turelem's teeth!" Bertrek exclaimed. "I had thought my aides were exaggerating when they told me about your face. Take off your hood so I can examine these markings." He remained seated behind his desk, so I took this as an idle request. In any case, I certainly was not going to let him inspect my face. Slow-witted though he was, I had no doubt he would recognize the captain who had once so thoroughly humiliated him.

"With respect, General, it is customary for men of my order to keep our heads covered."

But the General seemed to have forgotten his request already. "They tell me you were found wandering the plain. What is your name?"

"I am Samvel. I was not wandering, General. I was seeking you."

"Oh?" said Bertrek with a smile. "I hope you intend to entertain me with tricks. It has been a long day, and I could use some amusement."

"I do not use my powers for such purposes."

"No? A pity." Bertrek slumped back in his chair, sulking.

"General, I come to speak to you of a grave danger."

"You come from Nagyvaros?"

"Yes. The city has—"

"My scouts have already reported on the condition of the city. It's a shame, but what could we do? My division was occupied with a Barbarok incursion at the pass of Asztal. We got here as quickly as we could."

"It is not of the Barbaroki I speak. A powerful demon makes his way across the plain toward Nagyvaros. He and his horde will attack the city on the next full moon."

Bertrek began to look bored. "I've heard stories about this supposed demon. Residents of some of the villages to the southeast claim to have seen him."

"His name is Voros Korom," I said. "He comes to lay waste to Nagyvaros."

"He is a tale told to keep children from staying out after dark," Bertrek said. Having made this pronouncement, he nodded, evidently deciding that it was a perfectly reasonable explanation.

"Voros Korom is quite real," I said. "If he is allowed to reach Nagyvaros, he will kill every person in the city who still remains alive. With your help, though, I believe I can defeat him."

Bertrek waved his hand impatiently. "I was not commissioned to combat fairies and will-o-the-wisps. I am told the Barbaroki have turned south, and I must pursue them."

"I understand, General. I only ask—"

"You ask? Who are you to ask anything of me? A wandering sorcerer, or perhaps a charlatan? I owe you nothing."

"It is not for my sake I ask. I am sworn to protect Nagyvaros—"

"Ah, and a fine job you are doing! Nagyvaros is lost, sorcerer. Speak another word to me of that city or of demons and ghosts and I will have my adjutant cut your throat. I agreed to grant you an audience thinking that I might be amused, but you have only vexed me." He sat fuming for a moment. Getting control of himself, he said hopefully, "Have you not one trick you can perform for me? The journey across the plain has been hard, and entertainment is difficult to come by. I play cards with my aides at times, but I think they let me win because they fear me. One simple trick. Here, turn this quill into a goose."

I sighed. I was sorely tempted to pull the air from Bertrek's lungs as I'd done to the guard at the palace. A guard stood just outside the tent, but I could kill Bertrek before he even knew something was wrong. For that matter, I could snap Bertrek's neck easily even without the spell. I could draw the guard into the tent, incapacitate him, and walk out. I'd be a mile away from the camp before anyone knew what had happened.

But other than exacting my vengeance on Bertrek, it would accomplish nothing. Until I had dealt with Voros Korom, I could not take the risk of being apprehended. It was clear that I was going to get no help in that matter from Bertrek. I would have to face the demon alone.

"By your leave, General," I said.

"Eh? Oh. Yes, fine. Go."

I turned and walked out of the tent. A guard escorted me to the edge of the camp and I made my way across the moonlit plain to the place where Rodric and Vili waited. They were disappointed, though not surprised, by my account of my meeting with Bertrek.

The next morning, we traveled back across the plain toward the city. When the eastern gate was in sight, we stopped and set up camp. That night the moon would be full. If Voros Korom intended to take the city, he would have to get past us.

I laughed out loud at the thought. Rodric and Vili sat on the trunk of a fallen tree across a little campfire from me. The three of us were all that stood between Voros Korom and the city I'd sworn to protect. I wanted to tell Rodric and Vili that they had no obligation to stay, but I knew it would make no difference. They knew, and they would stay anyway. We would all die together. That was my hope, anyway—the alternative was to be assimilated into one of the collectives of wraiths.

I considered going to Eben in the hopes that I might still learn some way of dealing with the wraiths, but the last several times I had gone to meet him, he had not responded to my calls. In any case, traveling to Veszedelem and practicing sorcery would drain my energy. I wanted to at least be awake and alert when Voros Korom arrived. Rodric and Vili seemed grateful for the rest as well. We had done everything we could to prepare. After spending the day telling each other stories and dozing by the fire, we ate the last of the provisions we'd taken from the palace and then lit a torch and placed it on the top of a tall pole Vili had carved from a sapling. If Voros Korom came within a league of us, he would see it.

Shortly before dusk, Vili spotted movement to the south. We watched as a group of men on horses came into view. Had the Barbaroki returned? The group was coming from the wrong direction to be janissaries. Rodric picked up his bow, but I did not bother to grab my rapier. There appeared to be at least two dozen men, all on horseback. If they wanted to kill us, they would.

As they drew closer, however, I realized I recognized the men wore the ragged leather and furs of the Torzseki. The man at the front of the group, astride a beautiful cream-colored horse, was Chief Nebjosa himself. I hailed him with a wave. "Put down your bow, Rodric," I said. "This man is the chief of the Torzseki. He is no enemy of ours."

CHAPTER TWENTY

Rodric complied, still holding the bow at his side. When he saw the woman riding next to Nebjosa, however, he dropped the bow. "Ilona!" he cried.

It was indeed Ilona. She appeared to be well. I recognized as well the beautiful chestnut horse she rode: it was my own Ember. The group approached to within a few paces and began to dismount. I walked up to Ember and took her reins, cooing reassuringly to her.

Nebjosa must have heard the words I'd spoken to Rodric, because as he walked toward me, he said, "Hail, Konrad. Do not call me 'chief' any longer. I have been exiled from the Torzseki. These men disagreed with the council's ruling and have chosen to accompany me."

I nodded toward the men. Davor Sabas, the chief's advisor, sat on a horse to Nebjosa's right. "Decent and brave men they must be to have made such a choice."

Nebjosa clasped my hand as Rodric embraced Iona. "Brave or foolhardy," the chief said. "I told the council about the coming of Voros Korom, and that I agreed with your assessment. From what I have seen and heard, Voros Korom is a greater threat to Nagyvaros and to the Torzseki than the Barbaroki. They called me a coward to have refused to fight the Barbaroki, but they are the cowards. They delayed just long enough in their deliberations to render the matter moot. They chose a new chief, but not until the Barbaroki had already taken they city. And now they refuse to send men either to fight the Barbaroki or to stand against Voros

Korom. The men who accompany me do so as much out of disgust with such 'leadership' as out of loyalty to me."

"Your modesty has been your one failing as a chief," said Davor Sabas, leaning to take the reins of Nebjosa's horse. "I and the others would follow you into the Pit of Dravmal if you asked."

"Thank you, friend. See to it that Casimira is fed and watered, will you? Hayk, see to Ember."

"Aye, Chief," Davor Sabas said with a nod. Another man took Ember's reins and they rode to a spot not far away where the horses were being tended. The rest of the men occupied themselves with caring for the horses and setting up camp. There seemed to be about thirty of them.

"It is good to see you as well, Ilona," I said, and found that I meant it.

"I encountered Nebjosa and his men about ten miles south of the city," Ilona said. "He convinced me that I would not make it home. Torzseki scouts had reported that the Barbaroki were nearly to Delivaros, and they would have the city surrounded before I got there. I was willing to die fighting to save Delivaros, but I see no point in offering myself up to the Barbaroki on the plain."

"Then your destiny lies with us after all."

"Perhaps I have no destiny. I move about like a twig caught in the current of a river."

"You should not stay," Rodric said. "Voros Korom will come tonight, and our chances against him are not good."

"No, I will not leave the defense of Nagyvaros to a sorcerer. If I am to hold on to what is left of my faith, I must be willing to face the demon myself."

"Speaking for me and my men," Nebjosa said, "we will not spurn any ally against Voros Korom. I know little of such creatures, but I know that he will not stop at Nagyvaros. If Konrad's magic can be of use against the demon, I welcome it."

"It is the wraiths I am most concerned about," I said. "Your bows can bring Voros Korom down, but not if the wraiths kill us all before we can get close to him."

"And you have a way of vanquishing the wraiths?"

I sighed. "Chief, I have to tell you something, and you are not going to like it."

"That you exaggerated your power? I'm well aware of that, Konrad. I used you as much as you used me. I never considered the wraiths a threat as long as they kept to the ruins of Romok, but I needed a way to reassure my people. Hiring a supposed sorcerer who could tell me what I already knew was an inexpensive way of solving the problem."

"It seems I underestimated you. I apologize, Nebjosa."

The chief shrugged. "I was also quite aware from the beginning that you possess far more power than you realize. My people are largely ignorant of the intricacies of magic, but I know what that brand signifies. You have the power to stop Voros Korom and his horde. The only question is whether you have learned how."

"I do not know," I confessed. "I have been studying the properties of the arcane energy called tvari and practicing the use of it, but I will not know for certain whether any of my knowledge will do any good until I face the wraiths again. I think I may know a way to render myself immune to their attacks, at least temporarily, but that alone will do little good. Even if I could get close to Voros Korom, I do not think I could kill him with a rapier."

"Our arrows may be little more than an annoyance to him," Nebjosa said, "but we will do what we can to distract him so that you can execute the death blow. I would offer you horses, but we have only enough for our own men. Ember is yours, of course."

"I will not need her," I said. "I can stand and face Voros Korom on my own, and though I am certain she would stand fast, I would not put in her in so much danger if I can avoid it."

"Let Ilona take her, then. The animal has taken a liking to her."

Ilona shook her head. "I too will stand alone."

"If these two fools will face the demon on foot," said Rodric, "then I suppose I must as well."

"I will take her," Vili said. "I cannot ride and fight at the same time, but I don't suppose my dagger will be of much use against the wraiths in any case. I can at least serve as a distraction."

"Very good," Nebjosa said. "The boy is light and she is a very fast horse. If we can keep the wraiths confused, perhaps we will have a chance. Now I must ask you to excuse me. My men are hungry and tired, and we must eat and rest before the rising of the moon." The chief walked away to join the others in his camp. I counted the men: there were twenty-eight Torzseki altogether, including Nebjosa. I had hoped for five hundred archers, but they would have to do.

Ilona joined Rodric, Vili and me in our camp. The sky was darkening, and Rodric informed us we had about two hours until the moon appeared. Vili offered to keep watch, and I assented. One of the Torzseki already stood on a low hill to the east, watching for any sign of Voros Korom, but it wouldn't hurt to have another sentry. Rodric, Ilona and I sat around the fire, waiting anxiously.

The moon had not been above the horizon for more than a few minutes when Vili came running back to us.

"I see them!" Vili cried. "The wraiths!"

A cry went up at the Torzsek camp as well. Men leapt to their feet and began to saddle their horses. Nebjosa led Ember toward us. Vili took the reins from him and mounted her. "They're less than a mile away," he said, peering into the east. "Moving fast. I cannot make out Voros Korom yet, but the wraiths will be here soon."

"Then I must mount up as well," Nebjosa said. "Good luck, sorcerer. We will do what we can." He disappeared into the darkness.

I strapped on my rapier and Ilona picked up her stick. Rodric already had his bow in hand and his quiver strapped to his back. "What's the plan, captain?" Rodric said.

"Wait here," I said, pulling the torch down from the pole. "Things are going to get chaotic with all those Torzseki around. Stay near the fire so they can see you. Otherwise you're likely to get trampled. When Voros Korom is in range, start firing. Ilona, your stick is not going to do you any good. I suggest that you flee from this place. Go north, out of Voros Korom's path."

"I will stay," Ilona said.

I sighed and shook my head. Rodric shrugged.

"What will you do?" Rodric asked.

"I will go to meet the demon," I said.

*****

Vili rode on ahead of me. With the Torzseki aiding me, I had hoped to keep my friends some distance from Voros Korom, but Vili would not be restrained. Rodric could hit the demon with an arrow as easily from a hundred yards as from ten, and Ilona would be useless with her little fighting stick. It was a miracle she had gotten in a couple of blows against the demon at Magas Komaron, and the demon had barely felt them.

The wraiths soon came into view, darting back and forth across the plain, hungry for warm souls. Ordinarily when the wraiths encountered a living human, they would separate the person's soul from his body and absorb the soul into their collective, but Eben told me they would be unlikely to do this during a pitched battle. Assimilating a victim's soul took some time, and the wraiths would be busy defending Voros Korom from attacks. This was some comfort: those who died here this night would at least be at peace. I could only hope that Vili's eagerness to rescue his parents would not result in him being one of them.

I had nearly lost sight of Vili in the semi-darkness when Ember turned and came galloping back toward me. She turned sharply to the right a dozen or so paces ahead, leading three of the wraiths away from me. Coming up behind me on both sides was the sound of thundering hoofbeats. More wraiths flitted about some distance before me, to the left and the right. Directly ahead was the massive, shadowy, flickering, red-eyed form of Voros Korom.

I walked on as Torzsek warriors tore past me on both sides. Dozens of arrows shot overhead toward Voros Korom; a few may have hit their mark, but the demon did not flinch or slow. If he still bore any injuries from his fall from Magas Komaron, they were not evident.

Soon a half-dozen wraiths were chasing Vili, and he continued to lead them this way and that, allowing me to move within fifty paces of Voros Korom. Ember was fast enough to

stay just ahead of the wraiths, but she was running at top speed
and would begin to tire soon. The Torzseki remained just out of
the wraiths' reach, forming a circle of horsemen that moved
counter-clockwise around Voros Korom. The Torzseki, skilled at
using bows on horseback, continued to pepper the demon with
arrows while the demons surged outwards, vanishing just before
they reached the horses.

I was now within forty paces of Voros Korom, and the
wraiths Vili hadn't distracted had begun to take an interest in me.
Three came toward me from different angles, and I saw Ember
galloping toward me, now trailing nearly a dozen of the creatures.

"No!" I cried, waving my arms at Vili. "You've done enough.
Go!"

For a moment, Ember continued galloping toward me. Then
she abruptly changed course, throwing up a cloud of dust around
me. I heard Vili call something to me, but his words were lost in
the chaos. When the dust cleared, Ember was galloping away.
The three wraiths were almost on me.

CHAPTER TWENTY-ONE

I closed my eyes and pushed my consciousness to Veszedelem. Tapping into the tvari, I redirected a bit of it to my body and then pulled my physical form after myself into the shadow world. Then I directed some of my awareness back to the Plain of Savlos. I shuddered as the wraiths passed through me. Confused, they circled back and tried again. They could sense my presence, but my body was safely hidden in Veszedelem. They passed through me several more times, and each time I felt them like a chill wind, but they had no power to harm me. They swirled angrily about me, conferring in a confused jumble of voices about what to do. I ignored them.

The next part was going to be the real challenge. Eben had never directly answered my question about why I always appeared in the same place in Veszedelem. This seemed to be another secret he was keeping from me, but I gathered that this point served as a sort of mental anchor for me, in the same way that a grown man's dreams will often take place in his childhood home. Traveling the path of least resistance would take me to that spot, but there was no reason I *had* to travel to that spot. With some effort, I could cause myself to manifest at any location in the shadow world I had visited. By the same token, once my body had been transported to Veszedelem, I did not *have* to reappear at the same place in Orszag where I had left. I could transfer my body to Veszedelem and then transfer it back to Orszag in a different location. Because of the time lag, it would appear that I had teleported instantly from one place to another.

I had experimented with this idea while in the cell under the Governor's palace, with limited success. So limited, in fact, that the others had never even noticed I was doing it. I would travel to Veszedelem and then attempt to return to a place an inch or so away from where I started out. I had managed to do it a few times, but the attempts exhausted me. If I'd had more time to practice, I might even have escaped the cell, but I wasn't confident enough in my ability to avoid being wedged halfway through the bars.

I was certain that it was some variation on this trick that caused Voros Korom to appear almost as if he were in two places at once. He didn't seem to be able to teleport more than a few inches, and usually it was only an arm or a leg that moved this way, rather than his whole body. Voros Korom had certainly had plenty of time to master the skill, but he had had no formal teaching; it was possible that he'd never fully learned to use the abilities granted to him by his unique birthright. More likely, I thought, his inability to teleport longer distances stemmed from some natural limitation. A horse is naturally more adept at leaping fences than a man, but it lacks the ability to unlatch a gate. I was counting on my mental discipline and understanding of tvari to give me an ability Voros Korom did not possess.

Splitting my awareness between Orszag and Veszedelem, I focused on a point about two feet in front of me. Being half in Orszag and half in the shadow world is an unsettling experience because of the difference in the way time moves in each place. One part of you is aware that time is moving at an ordinary pace, while to another part it seems as if the entire world is virtually frozen in place. Even the darting wraiths moved so slowly that their advance was almost imperceptible. Having picked the spot in Orszag where I wished to be, I waited until the wraiths were clear and then pulled my body through. For a moment I thought I might not have the strength to do it, but teleporting on the open plain proved easier than in my cell. I found myself transported slightly closer to Voros Korom. The demon, distracted by the rain of arrows, had not yet seen me.

The wraiths, screaming in surprise and anger, whirled back toward me again. I waited as long as I dared, recovering my strength, and then winked out of existence again. This time it was easier: I was getting more adept at grabbing just the right amount of tvari and channeling it properly. Now back in Veszedelem, I saw that I faced another threat: the demons from the hills were once again racing across the plain toward me. I needed to wait until the optimal moment to return to Orszag, but if I stayed too long in Veszedelem, I risked being torn apart by demons. Not wishing to fight a war in two different worlds at the same time, I ran toward the keep.

Simultaneously, I reappeared in Orszag, a few feet closer to Voros Korom. He had been moving toward me, and now we were only about twenty paces apart. Arrows continued to fly at him from all directions, but now he took notice of me. He began to move faster, and he growled a command, pointing in my direction. I saw that his mutilated right eye remained half-closed. The wraiths harassing the Torzsek archers suddenly reversed course in response to his order and shot toward me. Again, I waited as long as I dared and then returned to Veszedelem.

To my horror, I found myself back where I had started, at the same place on the plain where I always appeared. I'd been so intent on moving toward Voros Korom that I'd allowed my concentration to slip. Several minutes had passed in Veszedelem, and the demons were now almost upon me. There was no way I could reach the keep in time to evade them.

I blinked back to Orszag a few feet ahead of where I'd left, barely dodging the dozens of wraiths who were converging on the place where I'd been a split-second earlier. In another moment, they would be on me. I could not stay here, and I could not go back to Veszedelem; either place meant certain death. So I did the only thing I could do: I withdrew from both worlds, pulling my physical form into the place-that-was-not-a-place, the in-between that lay on the infinitesimal border that separated the material from the shadow.

Once there, however, I found that I was still not safe: the wraiths were there with me. I should have known it, of course. The wraiths were trapped between Orszag and Veszedelem. I had unwittingly traveled to their home turf.

When I'd come to the in-between before, it appeared to be a place without form or dimension, but now I seemed to be clinging to the inclined wall of a deep pit, the bottom of which opened to an endless abyss. The pit was shaped like a huge funnel, its slimy, muck-covered sides streaked with cracks that allowed one just enough purchase to stand. All around me, man-shaped things moaned and clawed against the walls of the pit, trying to drag themselves to the top. There were hundreds of them, both above and below me, visible only as pale shadows. I knew them only from their howls, which sounded the same as they did in Orszag: these horrible creatures, I knew, were the souls of the people who had been absorbed into the wraiths.

Indeed, I saw now that there were not multiple wraiths, but only one great clawing mass of damned souls, all trying to get out of the pit. As they climbed over each other, some dragged others down in the attempt to get out. Occasionally one would fall, screaming, into the pit. Wherever one managed to get out, many others followed, and I realized that each one of the wraiths was really the manifestation of one of these streaming processions of souls.

The opening was far above me, and I knew that it was the way back to Orszag—a rift torn in our world by the presence of Voros Korom. At the bottom of the abyss was Veszedelem, and the pit was a conduit that had been formed between the two. But despite their yearnings to escape the pit, the creatures in it could not survive there except for the energy radiated by Voros Korom.

The pit, I knew, was not "real," whatever that meant in this place-that-was-not-a-place. It was merely a sort of metaphysical conduit between our world and Veszedelem. I knew, on some level, that I was not bound to remain in the pit; I could leave simply by forcing my awareness to a different "place" in the in-between, the way you can put one idea out of your mind and focus on another. But the more urgent one's desire to stop thinking about something, the more that thing dominates one's thoughts, and so it was with that pit and its clawing masses of souls.

I still might have succeeded in escaping but for the creatures' sudden interest in this strange visitor to their domain. I was at a nearly unreachable spot on the wall of the pit, but every one of the creatures nearby—above, below, and to either side—was now clawing desperately to reach me. Far above, others still tried to escape the pit, but most had decided to forego that goal in favor of easier prey.

As the creatures came closer, I saw that although there was some variety among them, they tended toward the same appearance. The one clawing toward me from my left was a prime example: pale, hairless and seemingly androgynous, with unblinking white eyes, it had been reduced from eons in the pit to something no longer human; mutated into a thing that existed only to strive forever at a task it would never accomplish. Many of the others were nearly identical to it, but a few still retained some vestiges of their individuality—lumps resembling breasts or genitalia, wispy strands of hair, sometimes even scraps of clothing. But they all clawed their way toward me, some falling in the attempt.

I tried to climb across the wall away from them, but my escape options were limited, and they came at me from almost every angle. I was reduced to pulling at their limbs as they came close, in an attempt to dislodge them from the wall. Their claw-like hands held tightly to the wall, but few had the strength to fight me; they fell screaming into the abyss. More and more came, however, and I could not dislodge them all. They clawed and pulled at me, and I kicked and punched as long as I could, but there were just too many. One got a grip on my ankle and pulled my foot away from the wall.

I fell—for seconds? Hours? Time had no meaning in that place. As I fell, I tried to shift my consciousness to somewhere else in the in-between, away from the pit. I felt a jolt and for a moment thought I had been successful, but then I realized I could still hear the moans and screams of the damned. I sat up and found myself lying in a pool of cold muck that smelled of sulfur and rot. The sky was a dull gray and the gray-brown swamp seemed to extend for miles. All around me, at varying distances, dozens of figures trudged through the muck, all headed the same direction. Turning my head, I saw their destination: on a low island perhaps a mile away there stood the ruins of what appeared to have been a temple. A warm, welcoming light glowed from within. Finding myself drawn to it, I got to my feet and began to trudge toward it along with the other damned souls.

I was vaguely aware that I had returned to Veszedelem, although it was an area of that accursed plane that I had never seen before. The sky was dimmer, and the muck, though cold and viscous, seemed at the same time almost insubstantial. It was like walking through the idea of muck: I could feel its pull on my boots, but when I looked down, I saw only an amorphous miasma of grayish-brown. I could breathe but could not feel the air in my lungs. Even the cold was more like a dull, sourceless ache rather than a genuine physical sensation. All the unreality of the shadow world was amplified in this place, and I realized the draining of the vitality of Veszedelem had been uneven, perhaps stemming from a particular place in this world. This swamp was evidently closer to that place. Was it the epicenter of the decay, or were there places even more degraded and unreal than this?

My mind rebelled against the dull, gray ethereality of such a place, and I found myself unable to resist the pull of the relatively substantial temple and the warm glow that came from inside it. Exhausted from my efforts at sorcery, I trudged mindlessly toward it.

From somewhere in the distance, I heard a call that rose above the din of moans that surrounded me. I turned toward it for a moment, but seeing nothing but distant silhouettes trudging through the muck, I soon forgot it and pressed on toward the temple.

"Konrad!" a voice called.

This time I stopped and peered across the swamp in the direction of the sound. A figure was moving toward me. I was about to resume my journey toward the ruins when the figure called my name again.

I watched as the figure approached. It was a woman, perhaps a few years older than me. She had probably been very beautiful once, but her skin had gone pallid and her hair had begun to fall out. Her dress was soiled and tattered. I did not recognize her.

"How do you know me?" I asked, still somewhat addled, and annoyed that she'd distracted me from my quest to reach the temple.

"Word has spread of you here. You are the one who carries the brand."

"What is this place?"

"That temple once connected your world to ours. It still does, in a way, but as you have seen, our kind can exist in your world only as wraiths. The light that glows in the temple is the light of the moon in your world. This is the only place in Veszedelem where phantoms such as we can live. The pull toward your world is strongest at this time. Most here cannot resist it, even though we know there is little hope of reaching your world and no hope of remaining there. Konrad, do you still travel with my Vili? Is he well?"

I could not speak for a moment. "You... you're Vili's mother?"

"I am. My name is Haneen. My husband and I were traveling with Vili through the Maganyos valley when we were attacked by the wraiths. It was many years ago, as time is reckoned in this place."

"Vili is well," I said. "I promised him I would see that your suffering is ended."

"Please, do not let any harm come to him."

Haneen's words had now fully disrupted my trance. "I will try. He is one of the few brave enough to face Voros Korom with me."

"You will not be able to defeat Voros Korom until you have severed the connection between our worlds."

"How can I do that, while the temple still stands? Is there a way to destroy it?"

"We have tried," Haneen said. "Arron and I and the others who have been able to withstand the pull of the light. But we are too few, and they are too many. Our numbers continue to dwindle as more and more are mesmerized by the light. Those of us who still resist have a small settlement here, but it will soon be overrun. I will not be able to resist much longer, and I am worried that Arron may not make it back this time."

"Vili's father tried to climb out?"

"He has gone several times. He is the strongest of us. He was not tempted by the light, but rather driven by the desire to protect Vili. It is one of the ways we know so much about you. It is how I knew you would come during the next full moon. But each time it was more difficult for him to return. I begged him not to go again, but he insisted that he had to keep the others from taking Vili."

"The conduit runs from Voros Korom to this temple," I said. "If we cannot kill Voros Korom, and we cannot destroy the temple, we are doomed."

"No," Haneen said. "There is another way. It will be difficult, but Arron has seen what you can do and he believes you can do it. He has been trying to get to you. I can tell you how to do it, but you must promise me that you will never tell Vili what you have done."

"I cannot make such a promise. I don't even know what you intend for me to do."

"The conduit must be closed, or all of Orszag will suffer. But there is only one way to close it, and it will not be easy for any of us."

"Tell me, then, and I will do it."

CHAPTER TWENTY-TWO

I forced my body back to Orszag a few feet from where I'd disappeared. Voros Korom was a scant thirty feet in front of me. Wraiths converged on me from all around.

With a tremendous effort of will, I once again opened a channel to Veszedelem. This time, though, I did not travel through it myself. Rather, I left it open and then opened a second channel, through which I traveled to the in-between. Maintaining my distance from both the pit and the channel I had just created, I used tvari to join the two together. There remained but one thing to do: I drew away a tremendous amount of the shadow substance from Veszedelem, infused it with tvari, and then released it in Orszag.

I reappeared a short distance from where I'd vanished, just as the kovet began to take shape in the sky above Voros Korom. It spread like a spidery cloud across the sky, blotting out the moon and plunging the plain into near-total darkness. The wraiths squealed as their power faded. I only had the strength to maintain a kovet of such size for a few seconds, but it was enough: the wraiths, desperate for the life-giving energy, were drawn to the dim bluish glow of the rift I'd just opened.

Overcome with exhaustion, I fell to the ground, glancing back just in time to see the wraiths surge through the opening and disappear. A few of those toward the rear seemed to sense the danger, but they were too close to avoid it. They were pulled into the rift like smoke to a window. When the last wraith had vanished, I let the rift close. At the same moment, the kovet dissipated, allowing the plain once again to be showered in moonlight. All was now silent except for the distant cries of the Torzseki and the flitting of arrows overhead. The wraiths were gone.

For a moment, Voros Korom stood towering over me, stunned and then enraged at what I had done. At least fifty arrows protruded from his flesh, mostly about his face, neck and arms, but he seemed untroubled by them. He strode toward me, bringing his massive right fist back to deliver a death blow.

And suddenly, Ilona was in front of me, holding her silly little stick in front of her like a ward. "In the name of Turelem," she cried, "stay back!"

Part of me wanted to pity her, but another part was angry with her for interfering. I'd done everything I could against Voros Korom; it was up to the Torzseki to stop him now. I had resigned myself to a quick, noble death. And now Ilona had gone and made the whole business into a joke. If nothing else, I thought, I had just proven conclusively that the only way to defeat a threat like Voros Korom was with sorcery, and here she was with her ridiculous stick and her invocation of Turelem.

Voros Korom must have sensed my annoyance, because he paused in mid-strike and simply stared at Ilona, as if amazed by her audacity, or at least amused by her foolhardiness. I waited for him to brush her aside or jeer at her, but a look of consternation came over his face. He drew back his fist again, but again did not strike.

"By Turelem's name, I command you," Ilona roared. "Go back to whence you came!"

The demon did not obey, but neither did he strike. He simply stared at us, apparently as confused by his inaction I was. Did Ilona really have some kind of power over Voros Korom?

The question remained unanswered as an arrow shot over our heads and embedded itself in the demon's left eye. Voros Korom howled and stumbled backwards. "Run, Konrad!" came Rodric's voice from behind me.

But I was barely strong enough to stand, much less run. Ilona helped me to my feet and we staggered away. The Torzseki, no longer kept at bay by the wraiths, rode toward the now-blind

Voros Korom, still pelting him with arrows. Most of these bounced off his tough hide; few of those that stuck penetrated far enough to do any damage. But some, mostly around his face and neck, had drawn blood. The Torzseki had seen this and were now targeting his head with more accuracy. Voros Korom threw up his hands to protect himself and continued to stagger away. It was only a matter of time now. Even Voros Korom could not outrun the horses of the Torzseki. As long as they didn't run out of arrows, they would take him down eventually.

But Voros Korom, apparently coming to the same conclusion, suddenly reversed course and began bounding toward us—and toward Nagyvaros. If he could reach the city, the horsemen's advantage would be neutralized and he could take cover behind buildings while wreaking destruction. He might even still acquire whatever he was after in the city.

Voros Korom broke out of the pack of Torzseki, moving at incredible speed. Ilona let me go and I staggered out of the demon's path. She put one knee on the ground, and for a moment I thought she was going to try again to ward the demon off. But instead she planted one end of her fighting stick in the ground, angling the other end toward Voros Korom. The demon's left foot came down and Ilona rolled aside. Voros Korom howled as his full weight came down on the tip of the stick. He tried to lift his foot, but Ilona had lunged back toward him, wrapping her arms around his ankle. Now off-balance, Voros Korom fell forward, bracing himself with his arms as he hit the ground. Nearly a hundred arrows protruded from his back; the Torzseki had continued to fire as the demon fled. Voros Korom lay dazed for a moment and then began to struggle to his feet.

I staggered forward, drawing my rapier, and climbed onto the demon's back, snapping off half a dozen arrow shafts as I did. My weight slowed the demon's rise a bit, but soon he would be on his feet again. I had one chance to stop him; if I failed, there would be no way to keep him from reaching the city. I gripped the hilt of my rapier with both hands and plunged it into the space between the two tendons at the back of his neck. There was a moment of resistance, and the rapier blade bowed so wide I thought it might snap, but then the point broke through the demon's tough hide and sank into his flesh.

And then he was gone. I fell to the ground, still clutching the rapier beneath me; the blade penetrated a foot into the ground before stopping. I pulled myself to my feet and looked around. Ilona stood where the demon's feet had been, her eyes fixed on me. Rodric was running toward her, and Vili was not far behind on Ember. Torzsek horsemen circled cautiously. Everyone was looking to me for confirmation that Voros Korom was dead. I wanted to believe my rapier had penetrated to the demon's spine, but I could not be sure. And I could not take the chance he might return some day. Fortunately, I knew where Voros Korom had gone.

Fighting against exhaustion, I envisioned the plateau in the mountains of Veszedelem where I'd been transported the last time I fought Voros Korom. Knowing that if my mental image of the place didn't match precisely, I might end up lost in the void, I pulled my body through.

I found Voros Korom lying on the ground, crawling toward his house. Gone was the baleful demon of a moment ago; Voros Korom had been reduced to a pathetic animal struggling to survive.

I was not faring much better. Trembling, I had to steady myself to keep from falling over. "Voros Korom," I said with as much bravado as I could muster. "It is time for you to face your fate." I reached for my rapier but found my scabbard empty. Even when I traveled to Veszedelem physically, I did not seem to be able to take anything of metal with me. I might have to kill Voros Korom with my bare hands.

"Leave me be, sorcerer," Voros Korom groaned, his voice strained and his speech slurred. "Can you not see you have already dealt me a death blow? I wish only to die in my own home."

I saw now that it was true. The demon's entire left side was paralyzed; I must have cut halfway through his spine. He bled from a hundred different wounds. I admit to feeling some pity for him at that moment, but there was nothing I could do. I did not have the strength either to help him or to finish him. Voros

Korom, realizing he was not going to make it to his house, had given up struggling.

"Come, sorcerer," he slurred. "Sit and speak with me."

I staggered toward him and sat on the ground near his face. The broken shaft of an arrow still protruded from his right eye.

"I am here, Voros Korom."

"I am... glad," Voros Korom slurred. "It is... not good to die alone."

"Why did you do it?" I asked. "Why did you seek to destroy Nagyvaros?"

"My... birthright," Voros Korom slurred, his voice growing weaker. "Invaders. Not their... city."

"The city was lost to your people long ago. You cannot fix the past."

"Would not have tried, but... Radovan... convinced me. Too... dangerous."

He was speaking so softly now that I could barely make out the words.

"What do you mean?" I asked. "Radovan convinced you of what?"

"The book," Voros Korom murmured. "Do not let him... get the book."

"Book?" I said. "What book?"

But I saw now that the demon's eyes had gone dull. Voros Korom was dead.

I sat for some time, recovering my strength, before returning to Orszag. I would have collapsed on the spot if Rodric and Vili had not been there to catch me.

"Konrad, what happened?" Rodric asked. "Did he escape?"

"No," I replied. "It is done. We have killed Voros Korom."

Nebjosa approached on foot. "It appears you did not need our help after all."

I shook my head tiredly. "We could not have taken him down if your men had not weakened and distracted him. I owe you a great debt, Chief Nebjosa."

Nebjosa smiled. "I am not yet ready to reclaim that title, but perhaps I will soon. As for a debt, you owe me nothing. The cowardice of the Barbaroki has ensured that I will receive my prize."

I nodded, understanding. With the Barbaroki gone and the gendarmes in hiding or dead, Nagyvaros was theirs for the taking. Much of the city's treasure had been taken, but it remained a valuable strategic location. Nebjosa could not hope to hold the city with twenty-eight men, but our victory would likely shame the Torzsek council enough to reappoint him chief. Or perhaps he would bypass the council entirely and appeal to the Torzsek people. A warrior who had defeated a demon and a horde of wraiths and who now promised an entire city would command considerable clout among the Torzseki.

I was dimly aware, too, that Nebjosa was letting me know in no uncertain terms that he considered Nagyvaros his domain. I had no desire to rule the city, of course, but the dying words of Voros Korom troubled me. What was the book he spoke of, and whose hands did he not want it to fall into? Nebjosa's?

I pushed the thought out of my mind. There were still too many unanswered questions, and I was too tired to even consider where I might begin to look for answers. If Nebjosa wanted the city, I would not fight him for it. At least not yet. The important thing was that Voros Korom was dead, and I was telling the truth when I said that we could not have done it without Nebjosa and his men.

"Very good," Nebjosa said. "Then I suggest we celebrate. We have wine and some beer at our camp."

"Thank you, Nebjosa," I said. "I am too exhausted from the battle to do much celebrating. I think I shall have to return to the city."

"Then we will meet again soon. For an impostor, you make an impressive sorcerer. I could use a man like you by my side."

"I will certainly give the matter some thought."

Nebjosa bid us farewell and got back on his horse, which stood nearby. He started back toward the Torzsek camp a short distance away, where the men had already begun drinking and singing songs of victory. Rodric pulled my rapier from the ground where it had stuck, wiped it on the grass, and then handed it to me. I took it and slid it into its scabbard. Vili led Ember to me and then he and Rodric insisted on helping me into the saddle.

I rode back to Nagyvaros, leaning against Ember's warm, damp neck, occasionally dozing, while the other three walked. After a time, I found we were back in the city. It smelled even more of death, but the smoke was not as thick and the chaos seemed to have died down. We took Carter's Ramp down to the Hidden quarter, found a stable where we could leave Ember, and made our way to the Lazy Crow. The Hidden Quarter was quiet; it seemed oddly untouched by the events of the past few days. We arrived at the Lazy Crow without incident. I remember Rodric helping me up the stairs but I passed out before I reached the room.

CHAPTER TWENTY-THREE

I was awakened by Vili, who was doing a poor job of pretending to look for something in his backpack. Vili was always as quiet as a mouse except when he wanted to be heard. Rodric stood at the window, looking outside. Full daylight streamed through the single window.

"Are you awake, Konrad?" Vili asked.

I grunted and propped myself up on my arm.

Vili came and sat down on the bed next to me. "I wanted to ask you something."

"Go ahead."

"What... what did you do to the wraiths? How did you make them disappear?"

"I broke the link between Veszedelem and Voros Korom."

"Did you see my parents?"

"I saw your mother."

"You did? How was she?"

"She was... Vili, she was stranded in that place for a very long time. It was not easy for her. But she looked well, for all that."

"And my father?"

"I... did not see him, but it seemed that they were both making the best of their situation. They were worried about you."

"About me?"

"Your mother asked me to make sure no harm comes to you. I intend to do that."

Vili nodded. "And what... where are they now?"

"They are at peace."

Vili bit his lip. I could see tears forming in his eyes, but he looked away so I would not see them. He got up and walked to the door, leaving Rodric and me alone. I sighed and lay back in bed.

"You look awful," Rodric observed.

"I feel the same. Sorcery takes a lot out of a man."

"Is it true? What you told Vili?"

"I did what I had to do, Rodric," I said. "There was no other way to stop Voros Korom."

"You said you broke the link between the shadow world and Voros Korom. But the wraiths didn't simply dissipate, as they did when they got too far from the demon. I saw them being pulled into a sort of vortex. Where did they go?"

"There are many things I do not yet understand about sorcery, Rodric."

"But you understand this. Where did the wraiths go?"

I sighed, realizing I was not going to be able to keep the truth from Rodric. He knew me too well. "They didn't go anywhere," I said. "I opened another channel between our world and Veszedelem, pulling them inside with tvari. Once they were inside it, I joined the two ends of the conduit together, forming a loop."

"So the beings that comprised the wraiths...."

"They remain trapped in the loop. I believe Vili's mother is still in Veszedelem, but his father is trapped with the others in an endless black tunnel. Those inside it could climb for a thousand years and will only find themselves back where they started. There is no way out."

"By Turelem," Rodric gasped. "There was no other way?"

"None that I know of. I only knew to do it because Vili's mother asked me to. I think she may have been a sorceress of some kind; she knew much of the workings of tvari. And she begged me not to tell Vili. What else could I do, Rodric?"

"Then neither of Vili's parents are truly at peace."

I shook my head. "Their souls were separated from their bodies when the wraiths took them. Their bodies died, but their souls were exiled to Veszedelem, in the same way that Beata's was. Vili's mother did not seem to have aged greatly, although many years have passed in Veszedelem since they were brought there. I think perhaps a person's soul may be immortal in such a state."

"Then they are trapped forever?"

"Vili's mother is trapped in Veszedelem until that accursed place at last dissipates to nothingness. As for his father… the only peace those trapped in the black tunnel will ever know is in madness. Gods grant them the mercy of forgetting what they once were."

"Truly, Konrad, I wish you had never met Eben and taken his brand."

"As do I," I said, "but I've been given no choice in the matter."

*****

An hour or so later, the four of us ate lunch together. Vili and Ilona were in good spirits, and Rodric seemed to have forgotten our somber conversation. Even I found myself smiling as Vili recounted the previous night's battle. When Ember had been too tired to stay ahead of the wraiths, he had retreated to a safe distance and watched the events unfold. He had an excellent memory, a sharp eye for detail, and a storyteller's knack. I was glad to hear him give nearly as much credit for the demon's fall to Rodric and Ilona as to me, but his account of how I had "put the wraiths to rest" made me shift uncomfortably in my seat.

Vili had spent some time that morning scouting the city, and he reported that the Torzseki had moved in en masse. Nebjosa had evidently made peace with the council; Vili said several hundred Torzsek warriors were now in the city and they claimed Nebjosa as their chief. They had taken the palace without a fight. The handful of gendarmes who had been manning it had offered their services to Nebjosa and he had accepted. Chief Nebjosa was the new de facto Governor of Nagyvaros.

Vili reported little looting; in fact the Torzseki, apparently acting on Nebjosa's orders, were doing their best to keep the peace. This was no doubt a pragmatic strategy on Nebjosa's part: he had more to gain by earning the trust of the city's residents than by taking what was left of its wealth. It was working. It would be a long time before the city was back to anything like normal, but when the Barbaroki left, it had looked like it would descend into pure anarchy. Now at least it was possible to start rebuilding.

Almost no one in the city had any idea how close it had come to being annihilated. Our battle with Voros Korom had taken place some distance from the road into the city; we would have to be content with the knowledge that we had spared the city from an even worse fate than being sacked by the Barbaroki.

We did not talk of the future. By this time, the Barbaroki would have reached Delivaros, making it impossible for Ilona to return there. I did not know what the future held for Rodric, Vili and me, but we would not leave Ilona when she had nowhere else to go. In any case, I had one thing left to do before I could make any decisions about the future.

I excused myself from the table and went back upstairs. I sat on one of the beds and readied myself to return to Veszedelem one last time. Before I could reach it, though, there was a knock on the door. I opened my eyes as Ilona entered. She closed the door and sat down next to me.

"I'm sorry to interrupt," she said, "but I needed to talk to you."

"What is it?"

"I've been thinking about what you said. About Turelem bringing us together. Do you really believe it?"

"No," I said honestly. "I was trying to provoke you."

"It worked. But there may be more to it that you think."

"How so?"

Ilona reached into her robe and pulled out a key than hung on a silver chain around her neck.

"What is it for?" I asked.

"I don't know. Eighteen years ago, I was found on the doorstep of the Temple of Turelem in a basket. This key was in the basket with me."

"You were an orphan."

"Yes." Standing, she removed the chain from around her neck and handed the key to me. I took it from her, turning it over in my hand. Other than the fact that it was made of silver, it seemed to be an ordinary key. Ilona walked to the window and pulled the shutters closed. They didn't block all the light, but the room was now dark enough that I could see the key shone with a dim blue glow.

"How...?" I gasped, holding it in my palm.

"It started doing that six weeks ago, on my eighteenth birthday."

"It never glowed before?"

"The acolytes never would have let me keep it if they'd suspected it was a magical artifact. Whoever had left it had known my exact date of birth, and had enchanted the key as a message to me."

"What message?"

"I don't know, exactly. A few days after it started to glow, I sneaked into the catacombs beneath the abbey, where the records are stored, to see what I could learn about my parents. I found the name of my mother, who lived in a village just south of Delivaros called Salonta. I went to find her, but she died six years ago. The landlord of the building where she had lived told me she had just showed up one day out of the blue, eighteen years earlier. No one knew who she was or where she was from. She was not wealthy but had a supply of silver that she used to pay her rent. She kept to herself, and occasionally she could be heard weeping alone in her room. The landlord said she overheard her say a name once. She remembered it because it was the name of a wizard she had heard about in a story a few years earlier."

"Varastis."

"Yes."

"You think Varastis was your father?"

"It makes sense. He fled Nagyvaros with my mother, but he either couldn't or didn't want to take us to Magas Komaron with him. For some reason my mother didn't feel capable of raising me on my own, so she left me with the acolytes."

"But with Varastis dead, you have no way to know what the key is for, or why he gave it to you."

"Actually," she said, "I do. I noticed when I traveled to Salonta that the glow diminished a bit. I thought that my father was using the key to lead me to him. As I traveled north of Delivaros, the glow grew brighter and I became convinced the key was leading me to Magas Komaron. At Almos, I turned east, but I noticed after several miles that the glow began to diminish. It seemed I was not being led to Magas Komaron after all. I was certain that my father was at Magas Komaron, but I could not find the way. I was about to turn back when I ran into you. You seemed to know how to get to Magas Komaron, so I decided to tag along with you in the hopes that I might still find my father."

"That is why you were so disappointed when you learned Varastis was dead. I'm sorry, Ilona. I did not know."

"Nor could you. But that is not why I confess this to you now. Although you are a sorcerer, I had a sense that we were meant to meet. When you said that you intended to return to Nagyvaros, I went with you, hoping that I might determine the reason the key glowed. The glow intensified as we got closer to Nagyvaros. When we were in the cell below the palace, it was so bright that I had to wrap it in my robe and sleep on top of it so it would not be seen."

"You think the key was leading you to the palace?"

"Probably to somewhere near the palace. Perhaps further underground."

My thoughts went to Bolond's song:

No one knows what Varastis found
Buried so deep under the ground
He left that night without a sound
For Magas Komaron

I had assumed that whatever Varastis had found, he had taken it to Magas Komaron with him. But perhaps it was too dangerous to remove from the tunnels under the city.

"Voros Korom spoke of a book," I said.

"What? When?"

"When he lay on the plain dying. He said, 'Do not let him get the book.' I do not know who he meant. Perhaps it was this book that your father found under Nagyvaros. He may have left it there for you to find."

"Then we must find it!"

"That will be difficult, as Nebjosa now controls the palace and the entrance to the tunnels. Even if we could get access to them, the tunnels are a labyrinth. We will need more than a magic key to find the book's hiding place."

"But we must try."

"Why?" I asked. "I understand that you may never be able to go home, and I am sorry for that. But you are a young, educated woman. You now have a friend in Chief Nebjosa. Your prospects in Nagyvaros are excellent. You have lived eighteen years without knowing anything of your parents or of sorcery. Trust me, you are better off knowing as little of such things as possible."

"And yet you pursue such knowledge yourself."

"I do what I must. I did not choose this path."

"Nor did I choose mine. Konrad, do you really not understand? I spent eighteen years thinking that all the world's problems could be solved if sorcery could be purged from the land. Then one morning I awoke to find that I possessed a magic key that could explain who I was—and perhaps much more. If the key was a test sent by Turelem, I've already failed. I think it is something more than that. I think it leads to answers I was meant to find. Perhaps you were meant to find them as well. This book must be powerful indeed, if it is what Voros Korom was after."

I sighed. Ilona was right: if the book was as important as it seemed to be, it was too dangerous to be allowed to fall into the wrong hands. For centuries, the government of Nagyvaros, with the aid of the acolytes, had strictly controlled access to the passages below the city. Perhaps they had known about the book, or perhaps they had simply walled off the areas thought to be too dangerous. With the Torzseki in control, everything would change. Nebjosa might decide that the ancient secrets thought to lie below Nagyvaros would be just the thing to help solidify his rule. And while I considered Nebjosa an honorable man, he knew nothing of sorcery and might very well unleash something he could not control.

My own motivations, however, differed from Ilona's. Having defeated Voros Korom, I needed to turn my attention to Eben the warlock. It was not enough that he remained imprisoned in Veszedelem; now that I no longer needed his help, I would see his soul annihilated for what he had done to Beata.

"Thank you for telling me all this," I said, handing the key to her. "I will give the matter some thought. Before I make any decisions, though, there is something else I must attend to."

Ilona nodded. "I understand." She walked to the door. As she left, she said, "May the blessing of Turelem be upon you."

*****

This time I didn't bother to go through the guard tower. Having mastered the ability of traveling to anyplace in Veszedelem where I'd been before, I projected my spirit directly into the courtyard inside the gate of Sotetseg. I made my way to the chamber where Eben had left the bell. He was waiting for me.

"Well done, Konrad," he said.

"You've heard of Voros Korom's death already?"

"Word of such event spreads quickly here, and I have access to more sources of information than I did when I first arrived."

"Enjoy it will you can. I have not come to speak with you. Summon your boss, if you'd be so kind."

Eben chuckled. "There have been some changes in Sotetseg since you were last here. I no longer answer to Szarvas Gyerek."

"I suppose I should not be surprised you have weaseled your way out of your deal with him. Still, I wish to speak with him regarding my own arrangement."

"You misunderstand, Konrad. Szarvas Gyerek works for me now."

"What? How?"

"An intricate set of machinations spanning the last several decades. I will not bore you with the details. Suffice it to say that Szarvas Gyerek is not bright, and I am persistent. Much work remains if I am to take total control of Sotetseg, but thanks to you, I have made a good start."

"You mean that the death of Voros Korom was part of your plan."

Eben shrugged. "I made a deal with an enemy of Voros Korom, to whom Szarvas Gyerek was indebted. When Voros Korom died, I became the holder of that debt, and thereby the lord of Szarvas Gyerek. But do not fret; If you had failed, you would have become a servant of Szarvas Gyerek, and I would have used you to the same end, although it would have taken longer."

"Your schemes will avail you nothing. I will see you destroyed."

Eben laughed. "You have shown a surprising aptitude for sorcery, but you know nothing of the history or politics of Veszedelem. Yet despite your threats, I bear no grudge against you. Help me now and I will give you what you really want."

"What is it that you think I want?"

"You want your life back. Give me the brand, and I will see that you have it."

"I care not for the brand, but the fact that you want it is enough for me to keep it from you. You cannot give me back my Beata."

"That is true," said Eben. "At least, not yet."

"Speak plainly, warlock. I have no desire to play your games."

"It is possible that Beata may yet be returned to you."

"You lie. I saw what was left of her fade when the red lantern was extinguished. You and Szarvas Gyerek told me she was dead forever."

"So I believed at the time. But since taking my new rank in Sotetseg, I have learned things that were kept from me. I believe it is possible to bring Beata back. Not as a shadow or a wraith, but Beata exactly as she was the day you saw her at the inn six years ago."

"I will not listen to any more of this," I said, and readied myself to return to Orszag.

"I do not expect you to trust me," Eben said. "We will make a contract in keeping with the ancient accords that rule this place, the same accords under which you made your deal with Szarvas Gyerek."

I hesitated. "And what do you expect in return for this sorcery?"

"The brand, as I have said. Also, to conduct the ritual to bring Beata back, I will need a certain artifact, which I believe to be hidden in the tunnels under Nagyvaros. It is called the Book of the Dead."

I wish I could say that I was surprised, but somehow I had known all along it would come to this. Eben was who Voros Korom had warned me about with his dying breath. The book was what Radovan was after, and the reason Eben had fought him. Perhaps not even Voros Korom cared about the city itself; they only wanted the previous regime out of the way so they could have access to the tunnels. So they could find the Book of the Dead.

I wanted nothing more than to leave that place, to never think about Eben or the shadow world ever again. I had spared the city from the terror of Voros Korom. Was that not enough? But I knew the answer as soon as the question had formed. Ilona was right: our quest was not yet finished.

"Tell me about this book," I said.

END OF BOOK TWO

Get Book Three Now!

The Book of the Dead will be available on December 7, 2019. Order your copy today!

The *Counterfeit Sorcerer* series is:

The Brand of the Warlock
The Rise of the Demon Prince
The Book of the Dead (Release date: Dec 7, 2019)
The Throne of Darkness (Release date: Jan 18, 2020)
The End of All Things (Release date: Mar 1, 2020)

*Titles subject to change until release date!

Review This Book!

Did you enjoy *The Rise of the Demon Prince*? Please take a moment to leave a review on Amazon.com! Reviews are very important for getting the word out to other readers, and it only takes a few seconds.

Get Email Updates

Want to get the latest news about sales and new books by Robert Kroese? Sign up for email alerts at https://badnovelist.com/get-email-updates/!

Acknowledgements

This book would not have been possible without the assistance of:

- **My beta readers:** Mark Fitzgerald, Pekka Gaiser, Brian Galloway, Mark Leone, Phillip Lynch and Paul Alan Piatt;

- **And the *Counterfeit Sorcerer* Kickstarter supporters, including:**
  A.J., Chris DeBrusk, Lauren Foley, Kevin Mooney, Bruce Parrello, Christopher Turner, Karl Armstrong, Jason, Brent Brown, Philip R. Burns, Eric Stevens, Josh Creed, Lowell Jacobson, Ben Parker, Michael Wilson, Robert Jacobsen, Keith West, Travis Gagnon, Dennis Ruffing, Christopher Sanders, Emily Wagner, Jad Davis, Grant Morath, Phillip Jones, Sean Simpson, Kristin Crocker, Slater, Ryan McGuire, Pamela Crouch, and Joel Suovaniemi.

Cover art by Kip Ayers:
http://www.kipayersillustration.com/

Any errors in this book are the fault of the author. I did my best.

More Books by Robert Kroese

The Saga of the Iron Dragon

The Dream of the Iron Dragon
The Dawn of the Iron Dragon
The Voyage of the Iron Dragon

The Starship Grifters Universe

Out of the Soylent Planet
Starship Grifters
Aye, Robot
The Wrath of Cons

The Mercury Series

Mercury Falls
Mercury Rises
Mercury Rests
Mercury Revolts
Mercury Shrugs

The Land of Dis

Distopia
Disenchanted
Disillusioned

Other Books

The Big Sheep
The Last Iota
Schrödinger's Gat
City of Sand
The Force is Middling in This One

Made in the USA
Lexington, KY
26 September 2019